The Towers, the Moon

Andrea K Höst

The Towers, the Moon
© 2016 Andrea K Höst. All rights reserved.
ISBN: 978-1-925188-10-3
EBook ISBN: 978-1-925188-11-0
www.andreakhost.com
Cover art: Likhain

Acknowledgements

With deep thanks to Judith Tarr,
Antoine, and KA, for much-needed assistance.

Author's Note

This book is in Australian English.

These short stories sit between *The Pyramids of London*
and *Tangleways* in *The Trifold Age* series. They contain
mild spoilers for *The Pyramids of London*.

Table of Contents

Two Wings

Griff Tenning, kneeling on his seat, strained to see through to the windows of the airship's forward compartment, but there were heads, a potted palm, and a very round man in the way.

"How can these be the best seats for viewing?" he asked. "At the back and on the wrong side?"

"Which is better?" his aunt replied. "A long view at a distance, or a shorter view right up close?"

"Both. They wouldn't even notice if I went up front."

"They did the last two times," Griff's sister Ned said. "I think they meant it about putting you up in one of the ballonet seats next time they caught you."

The insistence of the airship staff that passengers keep to their own particular quarter of the main gondola, rather than crowd to the best vantage points, was peculiar and unfair, but Griff had yet to find a way around it. Ever since he'd turned thirteen, opening his eyes wide and asking as politely as possible was no longer consistently effective. Unfair.

Deciding not to risk being stowed up with the second class passengers inside the outer envelope of the airship's ballonet, where there would be no views at all, Griff turned to his own window. At least they were coming over the city proper now, and there were streets, and rows of houses, all dressed up in tiny wrought iron balconies, too small to even step out on. Griff thrust his head out the window, and when Aunt Arianne quickly grasped the waistband of his shendy, he leaned further, drinking in the courses of the roads, and all the different sorts of chimneys. Lutèce, capital of France, spread out like a little map.

Airships were better than anything. You could see the city's bones from up above, and all the little secret places usually blocked by high walls. Best of all, Griff didn't really feel like they were moving, and so long as he didn't keep focused on any single object on the ground, he hardly felt sick at all.

"We're about to turn," a passing attendant said. "You'll see the Sun Palace almost directly below us, and then the Towers."

Griff leaned further, then pulled back a little when Aunt Arianne gave his waistband a warning tug. It was bad design that the airship didn't have a glass bottom. He wanted to see the palace from above most particularly, because photographs were not the same, and...yes! There it was.

France had a Sun Court and a Moon Court. The Moon Court – the Cour de Lune – was properly in charge, of course, but since they could only come out at night, the French had a human King as well. The yellow stone palace curving along the shore of a dark artificial lake was meant to represent a solar eclipse, to make sure the King never forgot exactly where he stood. This King. They changed kings a lot, in France.

The palace façade was a perfect curve, and there were exactly two hundred and twenty-two columns. Symmetry and repetition, not something that would be interesting if it was everywhere, but...

Stomach churning, Griff sat down. Aunt Arianne handed him a glass of water, and he took a hasty sip, then turned the whole of his attention back to the window, and just in time. One of the world's greatest wonders heeled into view.

"It's like a giant dandelion."

Typical Ned, with her head full of plants. "A snowflake," Griff corrected. "If snowflakes formed as domes instead of flat."

Though he saw where Ned had got the idea of dandelions. There was a central core, dimpled much like the round bit at the centre of a puff of dandelion seeds. That was the Hall of Balance, filling the Island of Emergence right in the middle of the River Seine. Out of it rose the Towers of the Moon. The central tower, the Tower of Balance, grew directly up: a single smooth column interrupted three times by horizontal structures, smaller columns spreading out to form interconnecting stars. The stars increased in size so that the largest was at the top, like a faintly curving snowflake suspended on a pole.

Four other major towers grew to the same length as the central column, but projected out at precise forty-five degree angles north, south, east and west. The stars of their three levels met and joined with each other, and with the stars of the central column, to form three filigree domes, each inside the other.

The whole thing was a deep black, though up close the black would have tones of muted, rainbow velvet. And that was just in the daytime. At night, when the Cour de Lune came, it would glow white and then really would look like a dandelion.

But more like a snowflake.

No human could build anything like the Towers of the Moon. The Towers had grown, expanding from the central core, and increased in size every year since the Court had taken France. The entire thing was hollow, filled with floors and walls and furniture, waiting for sunset when the Court would arrive. Griff began calculating just how many square miles it covered, and how long, at the known rate of growth, it would be before it swallowed the Sun Palace – for the third time in the Court's history – and they would have to build another.

Enormous as it was, Griff's view of the Towers was irritatingly short, as the airship curved around to the north-west and began to drop toward the ground. Griff continued to stare at the increasingly foreshortened view, but sat back as he did so.

"Le Tour de l'équilibre..." Ned was saying.

"La Tour," Griff put in quickly. "Towers are 'la', right, Aunt Arianne?"

"That's right," Aunt Arianne said. "The one nearest us is La Tour de ciel. East is La Tour de neige, west is La Tour Dorée, and north La Tour de tambour."

"The Sky, the Snow, the Gilded, and the Drum," Griff said helpfully, and quickly moved out of reach when Ned leaned forward to tweak his nose. "I'm not showing off, I'm *explaining*."

"Good that he can speak a bit of it," Griff's other sister, Eleri, said. "Even if obnoxious about it."

Griff peeked at her out of the corner of his eye. A little while ago, Eleri had stopped being Eleri, and had become someone who spoke a lot less, and moped over a girl, and was different and strange. Griff didn't know how to make her go back to being Eleri.

"You two will be able to get by on your Latin," Aunt Arianne said. "Tante Sabet is fluent – most people who have to deal frequently with travellers have some Latin, if grudgingly so, and the constant exchange of rule in Aquitania gives Latin a particularly strong presence in France."

Aquitania was the country south of France – or Southern France, whenever the French won it back from the Republic. It was Roman at the moment, because the Gilded Tower was in charge of France, and they weren't very interested in armies.

French politics was interesting, but not nearly so much as their buildings, and Griff turned his attention wholly to looking about as Aunt Arianne got them from the north-west airfield to Tante Sabet's hotel in the city's south-west quarter, which was not, sadly, within the bounds of the Towers, but at least sat quite close to the nearest outer edge.

The hotel had particularly excellent little balconies, taking a theme of flowers with four petals and doing clever things with the negative space. Otherwise, it was nothing special as a building, just a lot of levels piled on top of each other, looking across at other balconies over a narrow street.

"Hotel Lourien," Ned said, reading the small sign beside the closed glass doors.

"Established by Father's father's father's..." Griff began, but then hesitated, and was annoyed, because Father had told him this, but it had gotten mixed up somehow.

"Your great-great-grandfather, Guillaume Lourien, married Aude Beaumont, and together they took over the running of the Hotel Beaumont," Aunt Arianne said, as she paid for their taxicab. "They had seven children and your grandfather was the son of their third oldest child, Honorine. Tante Sabet married the oldest son of the oldest Lourien son, which means she is, strictly speaking, our cousin by marriage, not our aunt or great-aunt, but the whole extended family and a great many people who are not in any way related call her Tante Sabet. We all come battening on Tante Sabet when we're short of a place to stay."

Aunt Arianne paid off the driver and checked to see they had their suitcases, then added with a conspiratorial smile: "Brace yourselves," before pulling open the door.

This interesting warning fell flat, since the inside of the hotel seemed all very quiet and restrained. Bigger than Griff had expected, with a nice ceiling and sweeping staircase, and an arch to their right leading to a space that looked like it was someone's sitting room, multiplied many times over. Lots of low, comfortable chairs, tossed in with some small tables. A big shiny bar took up one corner, reminding Griff of a public house, although the people inside seemed to be drinking coffee.

Behind the foyer counter, a lady dressed in crisp black and white said: "Bonjour Mesdemoiselles, jeune homme," and glanced past them at the door. This had become normal. People kept thinking Aunt Arianne was their sister, and looked around for their parents.

Then a woman coming down the stair said, in a disbelieving voice, "Rian?!", and that was like a magic spell, bringing people out of nowhere to exclaim as well, and to kiss Aunt Arianne on either cheek and tell her, as everyone who had met her before did, that she looked so young. Griff watched the kissing with interest, picking out the people who kissed his aunt on the mouth instead, and one who tried, but Aunt Arianne turned her head just in time, and then, Griff thought, it seemed she might have stood on that man's foot when he tried again.

Unfortunately, Aunt Arianne remembered them after that, and introduced them to the lady called Tante Sabet, who was very small and fluffy, though her eyes were as sharp and dark as her hair was soft and white. She told them welcome, and to stand up straight, and then she kissed each of them on both cheeks as well, and it seemed the whole room tried to follow her lead.

Griff squirmed out of the onslaught as best he could, though one of those who descended was a red-headed girl maybe a year older than him. Her name was Josette, and she was Tante Sabet's granddaughter, and Griff did not duck his head so much when she took him by the shoulders and bussed each cheek. Someone his own age had never done that before, and he was surprised to find it only half as revolting as the rest.

Watching Ned glow pink after an older boy did the same to her was worth the fuss, anyway.

Eventually all the kissing and introductions stopped, and they got to go up the stair – Griff eyeing the wide curving railing with interest – and into rooms just one level up. The older boy, called Milo, carried the heaviest bags. He had an interesting face, narrow and all angles.

"Devant les escaliers," Milo said, as he put the bags down in a sitting room that opened out into two different bedrooms. That meant 'front of stairs', which didn't make sense to Griff, but Aunt Arianne smiled and told the boy that she'd always wanted to try it.

"My room's next door," Aunt Arianne went on, switching to Prytennian. "Once you're settled in, we'll go to dinner under the Towers."

She gave Milo money before he went, overriding his motion to refuse it. Griff had heard of tipping, though he didn't know it applied to relatives, and waited until the French boy was gone to ask what front of stairs meant.

"I've never stayed here as a guest before," Aunt Arianne said. "Only behind stairs, working for Tante Sabet." She turned a considering glance on them, then added: "Wash and change out of those shendies into your semi-formal wear. Skirts are challenging under the Towers."

She left them to go to her own room, and Griff paused briefly to explore the suite and debate over who got which bed, and then made short work of washing and changing. The tunic and long pants were new, a bit stiff, and Griff much preferred his casual wrap shendy. With winter coming he'd be stuck in trousers for months now.

Tante Sabet was waiting in the foyer as they came downstairs, leaning on a gnarled black cane. Her expression didn't change, but she watched them every step of the way, and though Griff didn't know all the words of what she said to Aunt Arianne, even Eleri and Ned would understand 'trois garçons'.

France was one of the countries where boys didn't wear summer shendies at all, and only foreign girls would think to wear trousers. Since Aunt Arianne was wearing Prytennian daywear – long pants with a knee-length skirt over them – she wasn't really dressed that differently from Ned and Eleri, but it was true enough that, with their short blond hair and up and down sorts of figures, Ned and Eleri did look a lot more like boys.

They were also pretending to have not understood, and Aunt Arianne was very good at sweeping on around interesting ructions, simply saying: "They'll have all the girls after them, then," and asking about the taxi that was to take them to dinner.

It ended up being two taxis, since Tante Sabet and her son and his family were coming with them. Griff rode in the second, with Josette and her mother, and the woman who had been on the stair, who was some other sort of cousin called Martine. All of them were inclined to pet him, which Griff was willing to put up with. He suspected Tante Sabet, in the other taxi, would likely tell him to sit properly rather than hang his head out the window.

It wasn't very far to the edge of the Towers at all, but the drive inward took longer, giving Griff plenty of time to verify some of the things he'd read about the Towers. The domes really didn't touch the ground at all. Only the central building on the Island of Balance did that. The stresses on the five towers that grew out of it, supporting all of the interconnected filigree, had to be immense, though of course that interconnectedness would also provide support.

The river and the Island of Balance were at the very centre of the three domes, but the taxis stopped short of it, not far inside the innermost dome. A great, circular parkland took up most of the space around the island, interrupted only by a scattering of buildings and a few bridges crossing the Seine to the Hall of Balance. Everything else at the very centre had been cleared away long ago.

Hopping out of the taxi at the very edge of the park, Griff craned his head back to consider the sky, very pale and crossed and criss-crossed by three layers of velvety black.

The structure wasn't even narrow: the filigree only looked delicate because of the enormous space it covered. Every arm and twist and loop of the 'snowflakes' was at least as thick around as a house, and the five central towers much wider still. Why it didn't all come crashing down under its own weight was one of the greatest puzzles of engineering.

Absorbed in looking, Griff allowed himself to be chivvied over to one particular spot in the enormous ring of buildings that surrounded the park. These were almost all hotels and restaurants with outdoor tables. Some of these had façades worth looking at, and so Griff divided his time between domes and towers and hotels until a plate was put in front of him.

His stomach was quite settled by then, so he dug in, gleefully listening to Tante Sabet refusing to respond to Ned and Eleri's Latin, talking to them only in French, and correcting their pronunciation. He was lucky to be sitting further down the table.

"What time of the day should I switch from saying 'bonjour' to saying 'bonsoir'?" he asked Josette eventually. "Does it change between winter and summer?"

"When the sun is no longer above, whatever the season," Josette said. "Why is it that you speak French when your sisters do not?"

"My father had a book of maps of cities all over the world. I took French at school so I could read it. Aunt Arianne has been talking to us a lot in French the last few days as well, trying to catch Ned and Eleri up."

"Ar-ent?"

He'd used the Prytennian word. "Tante. Tante Arianne feels strange to say."

"She does not look it, certainly! You would think her the same age as Milo instead of Martine! I have been waiting and waiting for you all to arrive and tell me everything that happened to make her so."

This girl probably knew Aunt Arianne better than they did, since Griff had first met his aunt only a few months ago. But a lot had happened between then and now, beginning with a hunt for their parents' murderers, and ending with the return of the eternal Pharaoh Hatshepsu to Egypt. Aunt Arianne looked younger because she had been tangled up with a vampire, between all the conspiracies.

This took a while to tell, and before he was done the occupants of the nearby tables had openly turned to listen, and even the waiters were lingering and making unnecessary visits. Griff made sure to talk as clearly as he could manage, while pretending not to notice. Prytennia sat at one of the edges of the world: not very interesting to most people, but everyone knew of Hatshepsu's return.

"Your accent is really quite good for someone who has never visited before," was all Aunt Arianne said, after he'd finished describing Hatshepsu's departure for Egypt in the form of an automaton his own parents had built.

Ned was frowning at him, but Griff didn't care. A friend of Aunt Arianne's had died before Hatshepsu had been revealed, and he knew their aunt didn't really like talking about it, just as Ned didn't like talking about how she'd lost one of her arms.

Tante Sabet started to ask something, but then the sky exploded with birds – mostly pigeons and starlings – and Griff ducked his head, even though they were well above him, and didn't sweep lower before flying away.

"The Shift is coming," Josette explained. "They always leave. It is the first sign."

Griff approved. Anything that made pigeons go away was a right and proper thing. He hadn't begun to guess so many were up there, perched on top of the filigree. Were the Towers of the Moon covered in pigeon droppings? And how did plumbing and water and waste, all the practical concerns he was learning to take into consideration when planning buildings, how did that work?

Josette, when pressed, said, "The Towers take care of that, like a tree."

"It is starting," she added. "You notice my voice, it sounds deeper? The air is thickening. Now the colour will change."

All along the curving stretch of restaurants, people were falling silent, turning in their chairs, heads tilting back. The sky above looked darker than it should so early in the evening: a bruised blue that seemed to swallow the filigree, and then to contrast against it as the Towers of the Moon began to flush white.

Griff's stomach shifted. He swallowed, and his ears popped, but it wasn't too bad. He had worried that it would be like cars and trains and all the things that made his insides want to come out. Good. He had wanted, above all things, to see the Towers of the Moon, but it was better still that he could properly enjoy why this place was more than just an incredible building, why half the world wanted to travel to France, because there was nothing so fun as night beneath the Towers of the Moon.

"I'm floating!" a boy cried out, and fell over in a strange exaggerated wallow.

It wasn't true, not quite. Griff carefully lifted and let go of a salt cellar, and it dropped directly back down to the table, but it did so with a lazy lack of haste. It was very like being underwater, without the need to hold your breath. Griff felt immensely strong, like he'd become a giant.

"May we get up, Aunt Arianne?" Ned asked and, when their aunt nodded, Ned moved like an old lady, holding on to Eleri for support.

Griff was not such a namby, surging to his feet and laughing when his chair sluggishly leaped away and bounced like a ball, while the table shifted ominously before cousin Martine stopped it. She was smiling, though, so he just grinned and picked the chair up carefully and then turned and put all his effort into one giant leap, all the way over the little row of potted greenery, and the path beyond.

He didn't land very neatly, and tumbled and wallowed, and then lay on the grass and laughed until Ned and Eleri came and got him up. He and Ned and Eleri had a lot of trouble learning to stay on their feet, and the best of times throwing each other into the air, those launching falling over each time they did so, but the one flung into the air dropping down like a flailing snowflake. Dozens, hundreds, thousands of other people were doing the same, all across the enormous park, beneath the Towers of the Moon.

Above, people were flying.

Some were people-people, just like Griff, but wearing strange clothing with silk panels from wrist to ankle. They came spiralling down after leaping off the top of the smallest filigree dome. That looked tremendous fun.

Others were maybe-people. If you died in France, you would be reborn in the Court's Otherworld as some sort of winged thing. Most were 'la clochettes', tiny people who spoke in bell voices. Others were larger, like a cross between a snake, a dog and a bat, and were called gargouille. And there were rarer, different shapes, and Griff did not know whether to consider them animals or people, since any of them might theoretically have been people-people once.

He was glad those stayed mostly overhead, anyway.

Only a single time did he see any of the Cour de Lune, the rulers of France. A little cluster of them passed at great speed, and went on to circle the whole of the dome. People with wings, not feathery or furry, but instead leathery like a bat's, with a membrane made up of little circles and ovals, layered and almost see-through, and coloured depending on what Tower they belonged to. The ones who flew overhead were part of the current ruling Tower, the Gilded, and their wings were all golden circles, like a shower of coins, or sunlight reflecting off rippling water.

"Tired yourself out yet?"

Aunt Arianne, walking in short, effortless bounces, came bounding up to where they had paused for a rest.

"You make that look so easy," Ned told her. "I somehow keep forgetting where the ground is."

"Some people, they can never adjust to it," Aunt Arianne said. "They lose their sense of what is up and what is down, and fall over at all times. But a couple of days' practice and you'll find it no longer so hard."

They were a long way from the restaurant, and Griff thought it odd that no-one had joined in, and only Aunt Arianne had come after them. He could understand that maybe Tante Sabet would find throwing each other into the air boring, but–

"Is Josette one of the people who can't adjust?"

"Josette is far too grown up a young lady to be bouncing about," Aunt Arianne said, sitting down cross-legged. "She is very nearly fifteen, and knows better than to act like a tourist, particularly in front of Tante Sabet."

"You mean that the people who live here don't – they have this wonderful thing and they don't *play* with it?" Griff did not know whether to be angry or sorry for the French.

"The Gilded Reign is all about play. But Tante Sabet grew up during the reign of the Snow Tower, when everyone was expected to act very restrained. She didn't have to adjust too much during the Sky Reign, but she is out of step with the Gilded Reign."

The four Towers of the Cour de Lune that took turns ruling France were very different. Father had said it was a mistake to simplify them into martial, spiritual, intellectual, and sensual, but that's how Griff's teachers had always talked about them. The things people were expected to value shifted along with the Towers, but Griff knew he would not want to change what he thought important just because someone else was in charge.

"Poor Josette," he said. "Living in the Reign that's all about having fun, and stuck not enjoying it."

"There's nothing poor about Josette," Aunt Arianne said. "And I suspect you would have preferred the Sky Reign. It's a pity that they won only a short portion of rule this cycle."

The competition between the Towers was judged once a century by the Tower of Balance, which played umpire but never joined in. Griff was going to ask why he'd enjoy Sky Reign particularly, but Ned had a different question.

"You said that drinking vampire blood hadn't made you as strong as a vampire, Aunt Arianne, but it had made you stronger, right?"

"A little. Nothing spectacular, I'm afraid."

"Does it matter to you if you behave like a tourist?"

Ned was like that: not nearly so interested in politics as things that made her heart race – and drawing her precious plants. But Griff didn't mind, since adding Aunt Arianne to the launching team made an enormous difference. She even let them throw her up a couple of times, before they started back to the restaurant, and was definitely overall in a much lighter mood than she had been since…since they'd met her at the beginning of the year. Not just acting like nothing bothered her.

Perhaps she was simply glad to be back in France. She had, after all, dropped everything to come to Prytennia after Mother and Father had died…

Griff didn't want to think about that right now, not on such a good night. There were other questions to answer.

"Aunt, why do people-people's ears and noses and eyebrows get bigger when they get old, but vampires' don't?"

"The vampiric symbionts try to maintain their hosts at an ideal state." Aunt Arianne lifted her hands to her ears, as if checking their size, and then laughed. "I am now picturing my most-irritating vampire master with enormous ears and a nose twice the size of his face. That would go well with his eternal bad mood."

"And what about the Cour de Lune? They can live longer than most vampires – do their ears and noses keep getting bigger?"

"Yes, but the rest of them grows as well, to match. That's the main reason they don't usually go outside the Towers in our world – the older ones are too tall to even stand at a normal weight, let alone fly."

"Have you met many? What are they like?"

Aunt Arianne looked up as a swirl of la clochettes passed overhead, like a shower of tiny bells falling sideways. "I've never been inside the Towers – far too expensive an indulgence. I've seen a few of the Court at the theatres, but I don't have entrée to their circles."

Aunt Arianne always acted like having money was a bigger adjustment than all the other things that had happened to her. Griff started to ask whether she would like to be reborn in a different body in the Cour de Lune's Otherworld, a thing Griff found mildly horrifying, but Aunt Arianne was covering her mouth, yawning.

"Time to go back to the hotel, I think – it's been a long day. We can come back here again another night, if you wish."

Griff did. The Towers were even better than he'd hoped, and it had been a grand day, worth the risk of coming into a territory where you turned into something else when you died. And luckily Tante Sabet didn't really seem all that sniffy about what they'd been doing, instead teasing Aunt Arianne in a grand way about acting even younger than she looked. He still felt sorry for Josette, though, for having to sit with her family instead of seeing how high she could leap.

They had to take a special chain-drawn tram out from beneath the triple domes, and the transition left him heavy and tired, like he weighed twice as much as normal. He was glad they were only one flight up, and trailed everyone else up, clumping his lead-lined feet.

"Tell your sisters, be ready an hour before dawn," Josette whispered, passing him.

Before he could even turn toward her, she had trotted up the stair and was gone, and of course Ned asked: "Ready for what?" when he told her and Eleri.

"How would I know? I'm just saying what Josette said."

"Better set an alarm for an hour and a half before, Ned, if we expect to get Himself here up in time."

"I'll be up before either of you," Griff told them firmly, but ended up being dragged out of bed by Ned, as usual. He never could understand how it worked out that way.

They were eating some of the fruit that had been in a basket in their room when there was a scratch at the door, and Ned opened it to reveal Josette, dressed in trousers.

"They're old ones of Milo's," Josette explained, when Griff pointed them out. "He's waiting downstairs."

"What we doing?" Ned asked, labouring over her pronunciation.

"You've seen the Towers at sunset – you need to watch the dawn come in as well, or you haven't properly seen them."

"You just want to bounce around when your grandmother's not nearby," Griff said.

Josette ignored this, saying: "We had best hurry."

He repeated what she had said so Ned and Eleri could understand, talking in whispers as they followed Josette down a narrow back stair and out a rear entrance. It had rained, even though the sky had been clear before and was clear again, and the rain had brought a chill that made it properly feel like autumn.

A shadow shifted, but it was only Milo. "Remember to wedge the door," he said, with a resigned note to his voice, and Josette hastily turned back to collect a folded newspaper and used it to stop the door from closing all the way.

"Now we must hurry," she said, shooing Ned and Eleri toward the main street, and keeping them moving at a brisk pace – not heading direct to the Towers, but at an angle that took them to the bank of the Seine, which was wide and paved and handily passed directly beneath a low point of the outermost dome, giving Griff a good opportunity to observe it as they marched steadily into wobbly footing and enormous bounces. They reached a small park not too far from the outer edge, with a good straight view of the south-west Tower and the two inner domes.

"Just don't try to jump the river," Milo said, and then repeated himself in Latin for Ned and Eleri.

"Do people really try?" Griff asked, eyeing the wide gap to the far bank.

"Tourists," Milo said, shrugging, then gave in to Josette's insistence that he help toss her into the air.

After a while, they switched to a race across the park, and then a game a bit like crack the whip, where they all joined hands and, using Milo as the anchor, ran around him, trying to keep their momentum up until the person at the end of the string spun dizzily away – and usually the rest of them tumbled over as well.

When it was his turn to be flung, only the embankment railing saved Griff from a dip in the river, and he clung to it laughing, and then caught an unexpected noise nearby, and held his breath to hear it better. Sniffling.

He looked down, and saw the embankment split into a lower walkway, narrower and closer to the water. There were fewer lamp posts down there, and it wasn't easy to spot the source of the sound, but eventually he made out a hunched figure by one of the chain-linked posts meant to keep people from falling in.

Grinning for what it would look like to Ned and Eleri, he immediately jumped over the railing to the walkway below. The sniffler looked up, and he saw it was a girl, maybe a little younger than him.

"Are you hurt?" he asked. "Do you need help?"

He could see that something was definitely wrong, for the dim light reflected off a slickness at the back of her dress. But she shook her head sharply and muttered something Griff couldn't work out.

The tone said 'go away', though. There were times when Griff wanted people to just leave him alone, particularly if he was on a train and his stomach had turned into a knot. But he could say that knowing Ned and Eleri would stay within earshot, while no-one seemed to be around for this girl.

"What are you doing?" Ned asked crossly from above.

"There's someone hurt down here."

"Ah?" Ned looked about, spotted the girl, and gestured to the others behind her before lifting herself effortlessly over the railing and wafting down. She walked right up to the girl and knelt beside her, keeping it simple by saying: "Je m'appelle Eluned. Et vous?"

"Comment vous appelez-vous?" Griff added helpfully. Ned's accent was *terrible*.

The girl shook her head, and in a thick whisper told them to go away. By then, the others had arrived, so Griff explained again, and was surprised when Josette, after a sharp look, simply said: "Chrysalide."

Griff knew the word – even Ned would know the word – though he'd never understood why the French used it, because it was not as if the girl was wrapped in a cocoon. But, just as a caterpillar becomes a butterfly, she was growing wings.

Milo had joined them down on the lower walkway, and took the girl's hands, saying: "Come up. There is no clear thinking in the dark."

The girl obviously didn't want to budge, but Milo slowly backed away, and she came with him rather than fight. They followed a ramp up, and stopped at a bench under a lamppost.

The girl's face was like a marrow, but that was because she'd been crying for so long her eyes had swollen up and her skin had gone blotchy. Griff would cry too, if his back was like hers, with two thumb-sized lumps jutting beneath the skin, like boils grown beyond any reasonable size. There were scratch marks all around the top of her shoulders, and she'd torn her dress a little at the back. One of the things had wept a lot of blood and clear liquid, and some of the cloth was stuck to her skin.

Josette leaned forward, peering not at the girl's back, but at her face. "Aimée Bouchard's little sister," she said. "I am right, am I not? Nathalie?"

The girl's flinch was answer enough, and she turned her face away as if that would undo recognition. Milo and

Josette exchanged a glance, and then they both looked at the sky. Josette murmured something low, before turning and bouncing away.

The expression on Milo's face suggested that Josette going off on her own was an unwanted complication. Eleri must have seen that too, because she bounded off in pursuit, not so elegantly, but just as fast. Ned had produced a handkerchief and offered it to the girl.

"Vous...fai..." she began, then grimaced and said in Prytennian: "Ask her if she thinks it would help if we pulled away more of her dress."

The reaction to Griff's translation was not positive, but Milo promised they would be careful, and eventually Nathalie nodded and bent forward. This allowed Griff to see a sharp, bony tip emerging from the leaking right lump. The left was still swollen to drum-tightness, and he could just imagine how sore and itchy it would be, all at the same time.

Ned and Milo worked carefully together, peeling and tearing, and the girl bit her hand and shuddered, but didn't make any noise until they were done, and then she curled down even further, so her face was in her knees, and her voice was all muffled when she spoke.

"How far?"

"The left isn't out yet," Milo said bluntly, though he looked very sorry for the girl. "But soon, I think."

He added something in Latin to Ned, which Griff couldn't follow so easily, though he got the general idea because he'd already heard how this worked: if both bits of bone poked through before the Towers faded, the girl would vanish as well, returning with the Cour de Lune to their Otherworld. Because she would have become part of the Court, unable to stay in this world during the day.

"Josette has gone for your family," Milo said next, back in French.

"They won't come. They hate me now. Everyone hates everyone now, and won't stop shouting and arguing, because of what I am, because of what that shows." She curled even tighter. "Une bâtard."

Griff leaned away from the girl, murmuring to Milo: "What's a bâtard?"

Milo pulled a wry sort of face, then said to the girl: "None of that is your fault. Your family is still your family, and even if they argue and fight, they would want to be here."

The girl shook her head, and murmured: "Bâtard," again, then added, "I am not Papa's any more."

Ned, to Griff's surprise, said softly in Prytennian. "It means a person whose parents didn't marry."

"Like the children of the Suleviae?" The rulers of Prytennia weren't allowed to marry, so all their children would be this. But Griff realised his mistake. Nathalie meant that her mother, despite being married to someone else, had had a child to one of the Cour de Lune.

Griff could hardly imagine what it would be like, to be where this girl was. To not only find out his father wasn't his father, but to be becoming...not himself. Not just taller and hairier, and thinking that perhaps kissing wouldn't necessarily be like two slugs wrestling, but someone with things coming out of his back. And the children of the Cour de Lune left – became not a proper part of the world – when their wings started. Like all the rest of the Court, they would fade with the night, but they wouldn't return until their wings finished growing. That could take years and years, so long for some that everyone they knew would be gone before they came back.

It would be like dying before you were dead.

Gingerly, because he didn't want to disturb her back, Griff touched the girl on her elbow to get her to look up.

"Who taught you to tie your shoelaces?" he asked. "And threw you into the air, and carried you on his shoulders, and clapped the loudest when you came first in a race? Those are the bits that matter. That's what makes someone your da, not anything else. Nothing changes that."

Nathalie's swollen eyes filled with tears, and she began to cry again, in floods. Ned somehow got herself in the way, so the girl could clutch her around the waist, though there didn't look to be any non-painful way for Ned to hug her in return. The sobbing finally caused the left lump to burst, and unpleasant liquid gooshed down the girl's back.

This was properly revolting, but Griff hoped it would at least make it a little less sore. He didn't know if he'd helped at all, or just made things worse, and joined Milo in looking awkward and peering up at the curving filigree arching over them, marking the progress of the sky lightening beyond the distinctly faded domes.

"*Nathalie!*"

Swarms of people, quite far away, shouting. They should look funny, trying to run-swim as quickly as possible across the park, but they were too frantic, and too upset. Nathalie looked up, then shuddered into Ned's lap again, but Milo uncurled her.

"Not enough time," he said. "Come. Let them say goodbye."

He and Ned each took one of the girl's hands, and bounced toward the swarm. Griff, following behind, could already see a difference, a strange greyness and lack of definition to the figure in the middle.

Then the leading edge of the trail of people met them, and there were hugs and kisses and an awful lot of crying. Nathalie was already markedly less there, but still, there was enough remaining for her to hear, to look up, when a man – too far behind to hope to reach them – bellowed across the park:

"Nathalieeeee! Papa will always be Papa. Papa will always love you!"

Then the last of the glow faded from the Towers, and left the park with just a lot of weighted-down wingless people, crying.

Milo, solemn-faced but practical, located Eleri and Josette, red-faced and panting in the trailing pack. "One drama is enough for the morning," he said, and diverted them back in the direction of the hotel.

There were an unexpected number of people out and about, looking tired and worn as they, too, headed back to their hotels. People who had been up all night, bouncing or watching the fliers or the special acrobatic performances, or just being light. Griff watched faces, and noticed that hardly anyone was smiling.

The Towers were magical and wonderful, and yet even when you weren't losing one of your family to them you would feel this flatness, this disappointment every morning, when the normal world pressed down on you.

"She won't know anyone there," Griff said, as they passed beneath the outer dome.

"They say the chrysalides are cared for most kindly, at least until their wings have developed enough to determine what Tower they belong to. Then..." Josette shrugged eloquently. "Then it would depend on how well you match your Tower, I suppose." She sighed. "I own, I am glad, after all, that my wings never came."

When Griff stared at her, she laughed, though not particularly cheerfully. "It is supposed to be a wondrous gift, after all, to discover yourself part of the Court. You live for centuries, you stay young, and you can fly. Everyone checks for the start of their wings, and twice as often if they happen to be angry at their parents."

The newspaper wedge was gone from the back entrance of the hotel, but Milo simply strolled around to the front and came through to let them in. They slipped upstairs, Josette vanishing with a wave. Griff, hungry once again, sat by the window picking over their fruit basket until Ned came and rubbed his shoulder.

"Buck up," she said. "We made things a little better for her. I'm sure we did."

"There needs to be a way to stop things *changing* all the time," he muttered.

"Things stopped changing, you'd never get any new buildings," Eleri said.

"Might be worth it," Griff said, since there were plenty of buildings already that he had yet to see.

France made change obvious and inevitable. Every day the Towers glowed and the Court came and went. Four times each century the Towers swapped control, and supposedly all the people started caring about different things, and if their king wasn't good at the new things, they got a new king, and... It made Griff tired just thinking about French kings, let alone girls who grew up and sprouted wings and stopped being part of their families.

He glanced at Eleri, and saw she was staring out of the window again with that expression she'd never worn until a few weeks ago. And they were all supposed to just get used to the new Eleri, like the French were supposed to swap from debating competitions, to the things that the Gilded Court did that people spoke about in hushed whispers.

Was Eleri still Eleri? She at least was right in front of him, and not faded into an Otherworld. If he could change anything back, it would be his parents, not his sister, and a whole summer spent wanting to do that hadn't made any difference.

Griff sighed, and opened the window, and then started planning the places Aunt Arianne could take them all, now that he knew airships wouldn't make him sick. If everything was going to inevitably be different, he'd best grab at the different things he liked, in case they too faded out of reach.

Forfeit

Arianne Seaforth had spent her summer acquiring wealth, responsibilities, and secrets. Not least of these was an ability to catch flashes of emotion from those around her, and so when her oldest friend and sometimes lover, Martine Lourien, suddenly flared with shock, hurt and dismay, Rian naturally looked about for a reason.

They were visiting the crammed and labyrinthine workrooms of the Sourné, Lutèce's premier museum, and although the basement halls were badly lit, Rian knew there was no-one nearby. At least, not anyone with a heartbeat to betray them to Rian's new senses.

"Martine? Something wrong?" She saw no obvious explanation among the racks of costumes, and the work tables festooned with pieces from the Sourné's Theatre Collection, all in various states of restoration.

"Ah, no – my mind is off in the...I was thinking of Milo."

Rian studied her friend's angular profile, but Martine bent to open the drawers of the desk that belonged in particular to her, and the dark wings of her straight black hair fell forward to hide her face.

"Since he's still hauling bags at the Hotel, I take it Milo did not win the part in Bonheur's company?"

Martine straightened, smiling as she always did at mention of her son, but then blowing out her breath in disgust. "No, and I was so sure that they wanted him! It seemed certain! But I have hopes of his latest audition, for he is perfect for Tesaire! It is not mere partiality that makes me say so."

"*Death and the Moon* is in production?"

"Yes, at the Voltari. Milo reads Tesaire *so* well. They simply cannot overlook him."

Rian could feel Martine's frustration, but also a good deal of confidence. The problem was not Milo, then. From the way Martine was checking and re-checking every drawer, it looked like something was missing from among the pieces she was restoring.

"Isn't something like the *Moon* desperately unfashionable now that the Gilded Tower is ascendant?" Rian asked, eyeing the contents of the desk. A wooden mannequin head, a pair of embroidered gloves, and an elaborate waistcoat. A line of typewritten cards identified them as pieces from the Léon Bonnaire exhibition.

"Bah. Why? It is romance, and tragedy, and skewers Rome. That does not go out of fashion. The actors, they will perhaps wear less clothing than they would have under the Sky Court, but Milo, he looks good without his shirt."

Rian snorted at this frank assessment, but then fell silent, and let the break in the conversation stretch as Martine continued to unobtrusively search. The collection bequeathed by France's great actor-playwright was more than extensive, but Rian did not need to puzzle out exactly what was missing. She knew her friend. Martine was not careless, and the loss of some prize of theatrical history would ordinarily spur her to decisive action. There was only ever one reason for that familiar pained betrayal: Milo's father.

"Martine," she said, keeping her voice even, uninflected. "What has Henri taken?"

(ii)

"Why couldn't Henri stay safely out of the country?"

"That is rhetorical, yes?" Étienne Boulanger paused in checking his reflection in the Tower train's darkened window to glance at Rian.

"He was established in Aquitania! A devoted patron, an adoring audience. A playhouse ready to set him up in any role he fancied."

"But Bordeaux is not Lutèce," Étienne said, with all the complacence of a born Lutècian. "It is particularly not Lutèce under the Gilded Court. You have no taste for the delicious, Rian."

"I like to see what I eat," Rian retorted, but that only sent her handsome cousin into peals of laughter, oddly deep and resonant in the thickened air beneath the Towers of the Moon.

"Or, at least, who," she added, with a faint quirk of a smile. "Anonymous games with masks sound all very exciting until you reflect on a few of the possibilities behind them."

"Does anyone on your Never list have wings?"

"No." Rian had never even spoken to one of the Cour de lune, let alone found reason to avoid them. "But wings will not necessarily make me like the person."

"And yet you go all the same," Étienne murmured, pausing for a long, evaluating glance. "What can Henri have taken from Martine that would send you chasing after him?"

"Does it matter?" Rian asked.

"It can't be money. Martine has never had an amount worth the cost of all this." As a light outside the window marked their slow progress through the tunnel to the Island of Balance, Étienne gestured toward the extremely expensive clothing he and Rian were wearing. Fountain garb: the newest Court fashion.

While Étienne's trousers and doubled layers of elaborate shirt and long-skirted coat were things of dark, durable cloth, Rian's dress drifted about her in an airy shimmer. Not a single garment, but four slips worn one on top of another, and fashioned of tissue-thin, faintly glowing and extremely sheer cloth – Fela, produced by the Towers themselves. The innermost was a transparent sheath that reached all the way to the ankles, with a single side-split for movement. The layers that stopped at the knees, hips and sternum were no thicker and, although they were looser, the silken cascade tended to cling. When a couple danced together beneath the Towers – with all the swirls and lifting involved in dancing in the unnaturally low gravity – their clothing would represent the stonework and the water of a fountain.

Underwear was considered gauche.

"And it's not as if Martine would *have* any amount of money for Henri to appropriate," Étienne was saying. "Let alone things he could sell to raise a worthy stake for the games. Everything else of hers he took long ago. But...yes, that's it. Henri hasn't taken *anything* of Martine's worth your while. But he's visited her at work."

"Let's not play this game, Étienne."

"Very well. Shall we talk of you instead? Young! Rich! Notorious! Three grand achievements in a few short months, and I do not know which I am to congratulate you for more."

"I'm hardly the first to enter into the service of a vampire," Rian said, glancing at her own reflection, and then looking away from a face where almost twenty years had been erased. "I suppose becoming Keeper of the Deep Grove is an achievement, though I'm still working out exactly what I'm supposed to do in the role."

The duties of Keeper were nebulous indeed, especially since they involved few set requirements beyond service not only to her country, but to Cernunnos and the Great Forest. The lack of explanation did not bother Rian nearly as much as the sense that she had spent the summer performing not out of choice, but tugged here and there, following someone else's script.

"Prytennian ceremonial offices are not interesting," Étienne pronounced. "But I hope you wallow in the resulting largesse at least occasionally."

Rian smiled. "Perhaps just a little. It's something to not be forever adding up how much everything costs – though I suppose I still add it all up."

"Yes, and when you asked me to what it takes to visit the Gilded Tower, you winced at every second word. Cultivate insouciance, cousin! Let the diamonds drip from your fingertips with no more than a bored glance – and oblige me by ensuring I am there to catch them."

"I think you will have to be satisfied with tonight's treat."

Étienne bowed elaborately, barely keeping his balance, but then said: "How is it, Rian, that Martine can be so clever and talented a person as to overcome disgrace and work her way from dresser all the way to curator of the costume exhibit at Lutèce's most prestigious museum, and yet still be fool enough to let Henri anywhere near the collection in her charge? Now what has he taken? No, don't tell me, I already know." In his enthusiasm, Étienne bounced on his heels, and had to lift a hand to prevent his head from hitting the train carriage's ceiling. "Even Henri wouldn't run about pawning part of the Sourné's collection, so it must be something he thinks he can borrow and bring back. And that makes it entirely obvious."

With weighty significance he took his mask from the seat beside Rian, and put on first the silver-patterned black cloth that covered his face from the nose down, and then the heavier black headpiece that sat like a low cap over his eyes and the top of his head. These were always animal-themed, and Étienne had chosen the traditional black cat design, with his brown curls hidden by a pair of ebony ears.

The headpieces were an old tradition of the Gilded Court, a constant maintained through centuries of often wildly differing fashions. The most recognisable item in all of the Léon Bonnaire collection was the mask he had worn to perform before the Gilded Court.

Well, the truth would have been obvious to Étienne as soon as they found Henri. No matter: her gadfly cousin could hold his tongue when he chose to. The important thing was to get the mask back to the museum before Martine paid for Henri's folly with her hard-won job.

Rian glanced uncomfortably at her own headpiece, waiting on the seat. Pressed for time, she had selected a mask at random from a wall swimming with feathers and empty eye sockets, only to find herself holding the stylised visage of a white serpent with scales of golden leaves to cover her hair. A rare pattern, and not something she could dismiss as coincidence since she had, only a few weeks ago, given her allegiance to the Forest God Cernunnos, whose emissaries wore the form of golden-horned snakes.

She touched the laces that would hold the mask in place. Was this tangle with Henri another instance of Rian the marionette, dancing to the tune of gods? But what could Martine have to do with the oblique challenges Rian had been set after becoming Keeper of the Deep Grove? Those were most certainly related to Prytennia.

Yet it was not as if she had left Cernunnos behind by travelling to France, for the shadow of the Great Forest fell over all of the world. Not sea nor desert nor even polar ice would take her outside the Forest's influence. Somehow, since returning to France, Rian's feeling of powerlessness had only grown.

Lifting the veil portion of the mask, she settled it carefully into place before adding the headpiece. She looked at the world through a serpent's slitted eyes and considered the dividing line between chance and arrangement. This was perhaps the greatest change to Rian's circumstances, far beyond youth, wealth, and strange powers. This sense of being moved about. A pawn in a game she did not yet understand.

"Go over the rules for me properly," she said, as the train began to slow. At least France's latest obsession came with explanations.

"First, always remain veiled," Étienne said, fingering the dark cloth that covered his face below the headpiece. "The veil – and your name – cannot be wagered, removed, or lost."

"To preserve appearances?" Rian asked dryly.   She already felt naked.

"To add a feather's breadth of deniability."

Rian shook her head. France under the Towers was a mass of contradictions.   The Court of the Moon played games almost purpose-built for erotic entanglements – and welcomed the offspring this produced into their ranks – but married women whose children developed wings often saw their marriages founder as a result, while unmarried mothers, no matter what kind of children they bore, were, as Étienne had put it, 'disgraced'.   Even with a human father, Rian had all too often heard Milo referred to as Martine's 'shame'.

"Second," Étienne continued.   "You are never obliged to join any game, but nor are you permitted to leave one midway.   Most of them have several rounds, and once you start one you must see it out. And that is where your stakes are most important."

"Tears of the Moon."

"Exactly."

The train's slow deceleration ended in a series of judders as the chain tightened. Étienne snatched at a strap to keep himself upright, while Rian maintained a firm hold of the handle set near the compartment door, and still only barely kept her seat.   In the near-weightlessness beneath the Towers it could be very difficult to maintain your footing, and even the relatively slow speed of the chain-drawn train could send the unwary tumbling as it stopped.

Once everything was still, Étienne opened the compartment door onto the very end of a softly-lit platform. The bulk of the other passengers were already out and moving away: a crowd swathed in shadows and drifts of moonlight, wearing the faces of beautiful animals.

With absent-minded courtesy Étienne handed Rian across the gap before continuing.

"Your goal is to win the Tears of others and spend them on a Forfeit – or exchange them for money, if you are particularly dull and boring. But the Forfeits are what make this interesting – they can be anything you have with you, except you name and their veil." Étienne swirled the long skirts of his coat, then executed a languorous twirl that sent him several feet into the air. "You bring into play all of yourself, all that you know, all that you might do."

"Up to a point."

"Yes, yes. A single Tear won't get you very much at all. But ten for a chaste sort of kiss. Twenty for a minor secret. With all hundred of my Tears, most estimable of cousins, you could ask for a forfeit of 'my time', and take me into a little side room to enjoy in any way that does not cause me pain or humiliation. Though you would have only half an hour at most, which really is not enough."

"Don't get your hopes up," Rian said as they approached the exit ramp, and he paused to pantomime mock desolation, before moving on with the swift, swimming step of someone well-adapted to nights beneath the Towers.

He told her of other complexities – most particularly the consequences of betting beyond your limits – as they emerged from the winding ramp onto the Island of Balance: a teardrop in the Seine. Ahead and above, the vista was dominated by three vast domes of snowflake filigree, the layers making criss-cross patterns against the night sky. Shivering in a light breeze, Rian turned to face the Towers and the dimpled central building that sheltered the entrances to the whole enormous glowing construct: the Hall of Balance.

Over the years Rian had walked to the island many times, craning her neck to try to take it all in. The five supporting Towers drove at precise angles from the island: one directly to the sky, and four marking the cardinal points at forty-five degree angles. The domes, held up entirely by the Towers, covered most of the centre of Lutèce. No other structure in all the world was so large.

Even the Hall of Balance, which was not strictly a building, dwarfed human construction. Like the domes, it did not touch the ground, but was suspended from the towers in an echo of the layers above: a semi-transparent shell that sheltered the tower entrances like a fantasy of spun sugar.

The train had delivered them to the western point of the island, nearest to the entrance of the current reigning Tower. Rian, grimacing as the breeze flirted with a dress designed to play peek-a-boo, followed Étienne beneath the curving outer rim of the Hall. She had no coat or wrap, since the Towers lacked cloak rooms. At least the fragile-looking material was durable, perhaps even harder to tear than Étienne's thicker clothing.

They entered a place of fountains and garden beds, where a cloud of miniature flying people swirled in chiming cacophony overhead.

Unlike most countries, France had not been Answered by its gods. The Court of the Moon had been completely unknown in the region before it invaded, and the Court did not claim to be gods at all, or even god-touched. They were, they said, not interested in gaining the spiritual allegiance of humans, but were simply annexing territory. It had been proven long ago, however, that the souls of those who died in France went on to the Otherworld that the Court ruled, to be reborn into the vast shoals of flying creatures that swirled across its skies.

'La clochettes' were the most common: tiny winged humanoids with bell voices. They served the Court of the Moon, but were almost a separate society beneath the Towers. 'Swift mischief' was another name for them, and Rian watched a handful make a darting sortie through the crowds of visitors, paying particular attention to those wearing fountain garb. Coat skirts billowed, veils lifted, and a brief demonstration was made of who was 'gauche'.

"Any other rules?" Rian asked, as they joined the end of the line being funnelled into the Gilded Tower. The sun had been down – and the Court in the living world – for nearly two hours, but the line was still long, for Forfeit was played only once a week.

"Hm. Yes, there is a rule of exchange. If you have won someone's Tears, but they hold yours, before any forfeit can be claimed you must trade back their Tears for yours – to whatever amount is held. You exchange your own Tears first, but then you can 'claim' a particular opponent's Tears if you wish, if they're held by someone else. And if more than one person is chasing that person's Tears, the arbiter will settle the dispute with a roll of dice or a coin toss."

Since this was very relevant to Rian's intentions, she asked for more detail, and he set out minor formalities while the line moved briskly forward. The Tower entrance was a massive arch with a gargouille – an immense snake-dog creature with a flat face – draped over it. But the Otherworldly creature merely watched impassively as Étienne held up their tickets and whisked Rian underneath its coils. And then they were inside.

Rian had of course seen paintings and photographs of the Tower interiors. The main shafts were echoing hollow tubes, occasionally crossed by bracing bridges. An encrustation of balconies marked the entry point to the lowest of the domes, where several Court members were drifting across or down, while one lone flyer rose to meet them with strong strokes of dapple-gold wings.

Étienne touched her arm, and Rian saw that the line of visitors was dispersing into a string of side rooms whenever an opening appeared. Very interested in how doorways would simply appear in the curving wall, Rian followed Étienne when one opened near them, and found within one of the Court, seated cross-legged on a padded block in the centre of an otherwise empty chamber.

People with wings. A simple thing to say, but it involved quite a complication to the skeletal frame and musculature around the shoulders and back. It gave the upper torso an elongated appearance. This Court member's wings were tightly furled, and rose like folded umbrellas well above head height, the light brown skin of the wing shafts glittering with a series of fine chains attached much like earrings.

Masked and veiled and yet wholly expressive of unceasing boredom, the woman held out a long-fingered hand, and Étienne placed their gold-rimmed tickets on her palm. Rian, troubled by a sensation that her weight had increased, stepped carefully forward in response to an impatient gesture, and was smacked on her nose by the thick card.

"Breathe in," the woman ordered.

Rian inhaled, and her veil shifted under the new weight of milky droplets attached to the lower hem. She touched one, and it detached from the veil, hanging from her finger as if glued. Not a single Tear, but ten, formed into a single droplet for convenience's sake.

"Thank you," she said, as the woman repeated the conjuration for Étienne.

The woman glanced back at Rian, and briefly mantled her folded wings, revealing connective membrane resembling a shower of golden coins. A member of the Gilded Tower.

With a sketch of a nod, the woman gestured at the wall behind them. The doorway, which had vanished without Rian's notice, reappeared obediently, and they stepped through to the lip of a vast drop.

The dislocation was jarring. They were no longer on the entry floor, but instead a third of a way up the long shaft of the Tower. The balcony railing was low and, while the gentle gravity and the shaft's forty-five degree angle meant she could probably skip unharmed down to the foyer, Rian still had to take firm hold of herself against the sensation that she was about to plummet and fall.

"Turns the stomach, doesn't it?" Étienne said cheerfully, and led her along to a broad bridge across the gap, and then into the lower assembly halls of the Gilded Court.

While the whole place was constructed inside the hollow filigree of vast domes, the halls were less disconcerting than the main shaft. True, the ceiling was a good fifty feet above, and curved to conform to the shape of the dome, but the floor was a series of broad, step-like balconies, with nothing like the immense drop of the shaft. It was a little like a gently terraced hillside, with a glowing white sky.

No trees, however. As with the brief airship ride to France, she was above the Forest here.

"I see finding Henri is going to be the hardest part of this venture," Rian said, eyeing the dancers, the drinkers, the clusters of revellers – and uncomfortably aware of those who viewed her with interest in return. "I'm glad I brought you along."

"It's not finding him that's difficult," Étienne said. "He'll be at the card tables. Do you have some plan for once we're there?"

"You go away before he recognises you," Rian said. "Even with that mask on you somehow exude an aura of Étienne."

"And you, who have never visited this place before, will sit down with a habitual gambler and somehow come away with whatever Martine has lost? I always thought you a woman of sense, Rian."

"I am a woman with a precious friend," Rian said steadily, but then smiled behind her veil. "And not quite a vampire. I can hear heartbeats. That will give me the tiniest edge, at least against Henri."

Étienne shook his head in disgust.

"The thing you must understand is that, unless you are a fool like Henri, Forfeit is a game you play to lose. That is how it is structured, because it is the uncertainty, the loss of control, which is delicious. What are you, my most esteemed cousin, to expect to play Forfeit and win?"

(iii)

Henri Duchamps was not strictly wearing the current fashion. His coat was cut in a shorter style, expensive, but just a touch shiny at the seams. His veil was mulberry-red. He wore no mask.

"Now what will you do?" Étienne asked. "It was the Mask of Léon he made off with, was it not?"

Rian let out her breath in a long hiss, more exasperated than she cared to admit, but then she shrugged. "I suppose, if nothing else, I can force him to tell me what he's done with it."

"Lost it to someone in here, almost certainly," Étienne said. "If you are determined to try to match him, I will look for it in the meantime."

"Thank you, Étienne," Rian said, and he chuckled.

"It is hours to midnight still, let alone dawn. There is plenty of time for me to enjoy myself. You won't be able to join the game until the current sets have been played, so watch the exchange of Tears. It looks like Henri is doing well."

This was true. Although he was not wearing the most recognisable – and most-copied – piece in the Léon Bonnaire collection, Henri's veil was decorated by at least fifteen of the ten-Tear drops. Not a good sign: it was important to regain the mask without the loss becoming public, but for Henri to be without the mask and yet in funds suggested he had lost it paying a forfeit.

Rian studied the tables around her hopefully, but although there were a few lions, two in the silver and black of the Mask of Léon, they all looked new. Copies based on the famous original. Resigned, she focused all her attention on Henri's table.

The old actor was like a lion himself, though the swept-back blond mane was thick with pale streaks. Rian – and Martine – had first met him when he was in his early forties and at the height of his fame, celebrated and feted.

Now...well, the skin around his eyes was crêpey, and removing the veil would expose a sagging about the jaw, but he was still a vital, charismatic man.

Rian watched Henri play, meanly – and pragmatically – pleased when his luck turned and he began to lose his little collection of Tears. She spared attention to the other players at the table – eight in all – marking the pulse of their blood and trying to capture informative changes when their cards were dealt, and when they made their bets. Her ability to detect emotion was far less reliable, particularly when she wasn't touching the person, but she did catch flashes – usually when a good hand was dealt, or the player embarked upon a daring bluff.

At the close of the game, Henri had lost four of his fifteen ten-Tears. The dealer, wings folded to hide their colour, but almost certainly one of the Gilded Tower, called a half-hour break – for refreshments and any payments of forfeits.

Rian did not follow Henri when he left the table, merely moving to observe another table while tracking where he went in the room. Conveniences – in, out – then food, wine, before buttonholing a woman in a tiger's mask. Not claiming a forfeit, merely seeing where charm could take him.

He had a beautiful voice, did Henri.

Arms slid around Rian's waist. "Are you sure you will not give this up, and come enjoy yourself?"

Rian firmly removed Étienne's hands, and, turning, caught a glimpse of widened eyes through his mask. Then he laughed.

"You always were rather dangerous, Rian. A touch of vampire only adds to the fascination." He held his hands up in surrender. "But I will behave. No sign of the mask?"

She shook her head. "There are very few of the Court here," she commented, gazing about. Members of the Court of the Moon grew taller and spindlier with age, so it was easy to spot them, even without their folded wings poking above their heads.

"Yes, mostly only the young and poor, or those carrying out duty service. They're issued a certain number of Tears each month, because of course the reigning Towers are always competing. We're just spice, wild cards in their games." He paused, looking around. "Well, on the lower tiers I expect we're mostly profit for the city coffers, or wherever all that money goes."

Rian wondered, watching a pair of Court members flying overhead. White wings. The Snow Tower valued a kind of spiritual asceticism, and the competitions of their reigns revolved around rather remote expressions of aesthetic balance. Did a requirement to gamble and pay forfeits excite or bore them?

"He's heading back. I will be a few tables away. Good luck, dangerous cousin."

Rian nodded absently, and then – once she was certain Henri intended to return to the same table – chose a seat that would not be in his direct line of view.

Almost immediately after she sat down the table began to fill. Rian was faintly surprised, because there had not been so very many uncommitted players in the area, but then noticed the folded wings jutting over the head of the woman opposite. To much of this crowd, excluding the inveterate gamblers, the greatest excitement would be found in winning forfeit from one of the Court.

The slender, brown-skinned woman, perhaps six feet in height, had her wings tightly tucked together, but the red-gold feathers of a firebird mask suggested she belonged to the Tower of the Drum. Twelve Tears hung from her golden veil.

A convenient development, for the winged woman would draw attention from Rian.

When eight players were seated, the dealer began to explain the rules of the game. Nothing surprising. The standard French deck of a hundred, divided into ten suits of ten. Pay one Tear to be dealt a hand, and then choose to either fold or pay two, then five, ten, twenty, forty to play on. Among timid players, only those who had a good hand would ever do anything but fold. For the daring, the trick was to read the table, and, if you judged that no-one had a truly outstanding hand, pay the increasingly high cost of staying in play until the rest folded, or the fifth payment round was reached. The game was a long one, divided into five sets of five hands, with forfeits to be paid only after the final two sets.

Rian spent the first set establishing herself as mildly adventurous: staying in play for a round or two even when she had an indifferent hand, but then dropping out when the cost to stay in rose past five. On the fourth hand, she bluffed to a small victory when everyone else folded early.

Her attention was all for the pulse in the rivers of blood around her, sorting the lift of a near-certain win from the heady rush of a dangerous bluff. Occasional flashes of emotion added to her store. Henri, on a good winning hand, was lazily self-satisfied. The pair who sat on either side of Rian were eager, titillated by possibility, as was one of those opposite, and the man next to Henri. The Court member seemed relaxed, while the man who sat directly across from Rian, hidden by a fox's mask and a green veil, discomforted Rian with a heavy hunger directed at herself.

In the past few weeks, since Rian had survived vampiric bonding, she'd more than once encountered that hunger. It was an interest that seemed to revolve around her apparent youth, which her mask and veil for some reason emphasised. When she truly had been seventeen she had not attracted such interest...or perhaps had simply not noticed it.

In any case, Rian doubted she would enjoy paying any kind of forfeit to this man, and was glad to remember the limits Étienne had described, and doubly glad at the end of the first five hands when everyone, as a matter of course, traded back as many of their own Tears as they were able. Thanks to her single win, Rian was only down two of her hundred. Now, with some idea of the invisible 'tells' that should let her know bluff from true confidence, all she could do was pay attention and hope for an opening.

The dealer gave the opportunity for a break, but no-one took it. In the second set, Henri maintained his Tears, and Rian dropped to eighty with an incautious bluff. At the end of the third she was up over a hundred, with two small wins, and had eight of Henri's. He was down to nine ten-Tears.

That was probably enough to gain the answer she needed. No great secret, surely, to ask what he had done with his 'borrowed' mask. Frustrated that there would be no claiming of forfeits until the end of next set, Rian could only hope that she could maintain her small advantage for another five hands.

They took a brief break, and settled back at the table with a sense of heightened anticipation that was likely due to the fifty Tears that the Court member had lost. Especially now that they had reached the sets that counted, where forfeit could be claimed.

Rian folded immediately in the first hand, and then bluffed and lost nearly two whole ten-Tears to the woman on her left. All the players were taking greater risks now, and few dropped out immediately. Rian stayed in with a moderate hand on the third, but lost to a better one, and did not stay past deal for the fourth. She still had Henri's eight Tears, but she would lose them in the end-of-set exchange if she did not regain her losses.

The last deal gave her reasonable cards, not brilliant. There was no spurt of pleasure from the other players to suggest any of them had had better luck, but Henri, down to seventy Tears, relaxed in his chair even as his pulse quickened. By now the combination was unmistakeable: he had watched their reactions to the deal, and decided to bluff.

Rian's problem now became the rest of the table. Two folded in the first round, but Henri, the women on either side of Rian, the fox mask, and the Court member all offered up two Tears to continue.

At five, the woman on Rian's right folded. Henri, with a wonderful air of indifference, took a Tear from his veil and tapped it so that it fell into ten. He flicked five of these into the centre of the table, and settled back. Both the man in the fox mask and the member of the Court also paid five Tears and the cat-masked woman on Rian's left, after a moment's hesitation, did the same.

So did Rian.

The Court member was a significant problem. Her pulse had not altered to any marked degree with the raising of stakes, and Rian's ability to sense emotion had not triggered at all with her – a not uncommon difficulty with those who belonged to a power outside the Forest. Rian's Sun-Moon-Stars hand was good, but there were a dozen combinations that bettered it. The fox and cat, like Henri, were bluffing.

At ten the cat dropped out.

The order of play now became particularly important, because Henri was first of those who remained: the best position for a bluff play. And he made a wonderful production of it, with a barely visible hesitation before he lifted a hand to the five ten-Tears still hanging from his veil and removed two of them. He paid them in with a slow flick of his thumb, and then sat back with a show of casual relaxation, even while his hands closed tightly on the table's edge. Trying and failing to hide nerves. And yet, in some ineffable way, exuding complete confidence.

Only that racing pulse made Rian certain this was not a man with a brilliant hand pretending to bluff, but instead a man with a bad hand acting his socks off. Henri's intense pleasure in the performance washed over Rian and left her feeling faintly soiled. This was what Henri played for. Money, yes, but more than that: a glory in his own brilliance.

Fox mask folded, which did not surprise Rian at all. The member of the Court played on.

Now came real risk. The woman was completely relaxed, watching Rian through the firebird mask as if there were no surprises in the world. The members of the Court had abilities linked to their Towers, but none that should give them an advantage at a game of cards. The Tower of the Drum had strength – such that the younger members were able to venture outside the low gravity of the Towers – and the Gilded could mesmerise. The Snow Tower controlled temperature and the Sky Tower could manipulate light. And all of the members of the Court could create certain objects, like the Tears.

"Mademoiselle?"

The dealer had been waiting too long for her bet. Rian thought a moment more, then paid in her two ten-Tears. Henri's bluff had already failed – he did not have the forty Tears needed to play further, while Rian could stay in and just manage to keep the eight Tears of Henri's she'd won, even if the Court member won the hand. But most likely no-one would play on, and so the three remaining would split the pot.

Henri, with every appearance of unalloyed delight, paid in every remaining Tear he owned, and then flicked his fingers at the dealer, murmuring: "Soleil."

She'd underestimated him. Not his hand. He was bluffing, Rian was completely certain of that. But he was the breed of gambler who would take matters right to the edge, and then step beyond, bringing into play a Tear of the Sun – a bet beyond his limits – to bridge the tiny shortfall in his stakes.

The dealer gestured, and a mote of golden light dropped into Henri's hand. He flicked it into the centre without hesitation, and sat back with the air of everything being now accomplished. Only someone with an unassailable hand would dream of paying forty Tears to test that apparent confidence.

The Court member folded, sparing Rian any number of tenterhooks. And Rian, who had no taste for torture, did not draw matters out, adding four ten-Tears to the glimmering centre pile.

"Thus the reveal," the dealer murmured, and Henri Duchamps was done.

(iv)

Every Tear of the Sun equalled a debt to the Tower of a hundred Tears of the Moon. Henri had paid a steep price for that final bluff, and Rian, more than aware of the man's chagrin and anger, was glad of the minor end-of-set business of exchanges that delayed moving on.

Accepting the compliments of the cat-masked player with a nod, she kept her reaction as tamped down as possible, simply ensuring she ended the trades with all of her original Tears – and all of Henri's.

"And now," said the dealer, "there is fifteen minutes before we recommence. Are there to be any forfeits claimed?"

The cat-mask player immediately claimed forfeit from the Court of the Moon player, and Rian said, very carefully: "I will claim from the maskless one."

Perhaps it was the steely note to her voice that changed Henri's dominant emotion to one of wariness. Or recognition. In any case, he looked at her sharply, before assuming an air of mild gratification.

"Any other claims?" the dealer asked, but gained no response. "Then the next set will commence in fifteen minutes."

Rian's ever-constant awareness of blood warned her of the descent of two people from above, but the only other warning was a faint disturbance of air behind her. She turned and looked up into the faces of two members of the Court that were neither masked nor veiled, and who were dressed in simple tunics and trousers. Their wings, still spread, were dappled curtains of black and deep purple. Arbiters of the Tower of Balance.

The one immediately behind Rian was a very pale woman, with a great deal of loose hair the colour of champagne. It drifted in sinuous rills, settling slowly downward in the gentle gravity, and had not quite finished its fall when the woman touched Rian's arm and they moved to another place.

The Tower of Balance owned two abilities not given to other members of the Court: translocation, and the power to 'follow lines of consequence'. This was not quite the same as seeing the future, apparently, but instead involved navigating possibility.

The pale-haired Court member had brought Rian and Henri to a room where only the floor glowed with the steady light of the Towers' outer walls. Rian was still seated, on the opposite side of a small table from Henri, with the Court member standing to her right, and Rian's collection of Tears laid out on the table between them.

Henri, who had been gazing at Rian through narrowed eyes, said in a richly enunciated and highly disgusted voice: "I should have known."

"You probably should have, Henri," Rian said, eternally weary of him. "I wish you would leave Martine alone."

"Is that the forfeit you request?" asked the Court member.

Henri laughed. "She'd not thank you for that."

"No," Rian said, despite a moment's extreme temptation. "I am here for the Mask of Léon, of course. What have you done with it, Henri?"

She could not see the lower half of his face, but was certain his mouth twisted into a bitter smirk.

"I will at least enjoy knowing you're on a fool's errand."

Rian looked up at the member of the Court. The dim lighting from the floor threw shadows of distortion over the woman's face, making it difficult to read her expression, but she waited with seeming indifference. The Tower of Balance did not permit gossip about arbitration, and supposedly anything done here would go no further.

"I want him to tell me what he did with the Mask of Léon. That is my forfeit."

"This is the cost," the arbiter said, and fifteen Tears lifted from the table, surprising Rian, since Étienne had said that a simple question would only be a few Tears. But, for Martine at least, this was not a matter of 'low import'.

Accepting the payment with the faintest nod, Rian turned her attention back to Henri.

"I surrendered the Mask of Léon as forfeit to Lionel D'Argent," Henri said. "Two hours ago."

His voice was flat, uninflected, and Rian shivered to hear it. This was exactly why she did not find the idea of Forfeit 'delicious'. If you did not pay your forfeit willingly, you still paid it. That was the power of the Tears.

Then Henri snorted, adding: "And much good that will do you. I heard you had come into money: how much will you throw away on a raw-boned nag?"

Rian only looked at him, her hatred cold, unstirred, for she had long known that Henri cherished not one ounce of affection for Martine, not at the beginning, nor after so many years and so much sacrifice. She had no idea who this Lionel was, but she expected Étienne would, or would be able to find out.

Even so, she glanced up at the arbiter: "Is it permitted to take more than one forfeit?"

"Yes, throw it all away," Henri jeered, as the arbiter nodded. "Beggar yourself."

"A binding promise, then," Rian said.

"You think she won't know? What will you say if she asks what forfeits you took?" Henri didn't seem to know whether to gloat or be furious. "These things," he added meaningfully, "have a way of coming out."

Rian shook her head. "I wish the world were so simple that I could force you to stay away from Martine and that would fix everything. But I can't make that decision for her. No, Henri, what I want is for you to stay out of Milo's career. Don't help it. Don't hinder it."

She had guessed correctly. He did not quite manage to hide the split-second fury, and she felt it roiling below the surface even as his face smoothed and he waved a hand in apparent indifference.

"I've already refused to put that brat forward. He has to stand on his own feet if he expects to live up to me."

"This is the cost." All but two of Henri's remaining Tears rose from the table, including the Tear of the Sun.

Rian accepted with barely a glance, head swimming with the hatred beating at her. She had never understood how anyone could love this spiteful, self-involved creature, but Martine did. If Rian tried to keep him from her friend, he would most definitely go out of his way to make sure Martine knew it, for he considered Martine a resource marked for his use. Not a friend, or his lover, but a fall-back source of money and sex.

And there was the problem.

She turned once again to the impassive Court member.

"He has no Tears left. What happens during the last set?"

"A player may stake anything carried or worn, except the veil. If the value of those items is exceeded, each action takes a Tear of the Sun."

The end result: humiliation. And probably a greater plunge into debt. Henri already owed the Gilded Tower the cost of one Tear of the Sun, and to escape what was likely to be a less-than-pleasant period of service, he would need an enormous amount of money, fast.

Rian was all too familiar with the consequences of Henri Duchamps needing money.

"Can I give him Tears?" she asked, failing to quite repress a heavy sigh.

The arbiter nodded.

Rian had started the last hand with eighty-five Tears of the Moon, and had gained one hundred and forty-four, along with the Tear of the Sun, which was worth a hundred

Tears of the Moon. After everything she'd just spent, she now had a hundred and fourteen Tears left. If she used a hundred to buy back Henri's debt, and gave him five to pay the cost of the deals, she would be left with nine.

It would mean abandoning any hope of finding this Lionel person and attempting to gain the mask back with another forfeit. Not that night.

Resigned, Rian paid over the Tears. She couldn't decide what to do about the mask until she knew more about the man who had it, but she was absolutely sure that drastically increasing Henri's debt was a bad idea.

Not expecting gratitude, Rian was unsurprised when he merely swept up the five Tears with a grunt – and possibly an irritated click of his tongue. Rian retrieved her tiny remainder, said to the Court member: "That is all, thank you," and had barely finished the sentence before she found herself back in the great, curving room, seated at the original table.

Henri, the only other occupant, flung himself out of his chair and stalked off. Rian, after a moment's pause, took herself to the conveniences to wash her face and rid herself of the question of how long it would have taken to earn the money she had just thrown away on a man she despised.

Étienne was waiting on her return, his entire stance a question.

"Lionel D'Argent," she said, wasting no time, for the break had only been fifteen minutes. "Do you know who that is?"

His reaction told her the news was bad.

"Oh, yes," he said. "I'd heard he comes to the lower tier sometimes."

"And?"

"One of Princess Heloise's myrmidons. He's been lurking around the Sun Court the last few years, and there's not much more I can tell you, since the name's obviously an alias. I can look about for him, if you wish, but chances are, if you want to find him tonight, you'd need to get to–"

"The middle tier."

(v)

Wealth was a very relative concept. Large portions of Rian's life had been lived hand-to-mouth: at first because her parents' income had been inconsistent and badly managed. Her father would buy extravagances, or work for apples, and her mother's reputation as a sculptor had not quite balanced the amount of time her pieces took to produce.

After their deaths, Rian had chosen to travel, and in many countries unmarried women had very limited choices when it came to earning money, few of which paid at all well. But through careful research, and a network of friends and relatives, she had found steady employment as everything from grape picker to archivist, occasionally falling back on Tante Sabet to give her maid work at the family hotel. Even so, nearly two decades of saving and careful investment had barely built up an income to cover Rian's basic expenses, let alone those of the nephew and two nieces left to her care.

Since her vampiric master had arranged for her the position of Keeper of the Deep Grove – a role that had come with an enormous house, a formidable yearly stipend, and even a hidden stockpile of money and valuables – Rian could not see herself as anything but wealthy. But it would drain her reserves to purchase the Tears of the Night Étienne told her were used on the Towers' middle tier, even if she had all that money with her.

And it would still not be enough, because to enter the middle tier, you had to be invited.

Rian, who more than once had had demonstrated to her matters of place and standing, knew perfectly well that the truly rich would consider her generous competence play money, and that as the undistinguished child of a pair of notable artists, she did not receive invitations to anything. As Keeper of the Deep Grove...well, in France that counted for nothing in particular.

As a Lourien, however, she had connections she could draw upon. Tante Sabet would be able to tell her of anyone in their extended family who had access to the Sun Palace, and might be able to reach this Lionel D'Argent. There had to be a way to arrange a meeting: if nothing else, palaces never exhausted their need for someone to clean them.

Preoccupied, Rian played through the last set with barely a glance at her cards, since she didn't have the Tears to win any hand where the other players did not immediately fold. She felt only vague relief when Henri did the same.

When the set ended, she looked about for Étienne, who had promised to scout the area for D'Argent. He caught her eye, and raised empty hands. Nothing.

"I will claim from Mademoiselle Serpent."

It took several beats for Rian to connect this quiet statement with herself. She looked away from Étienne and focused on the Court member in the firebird mask. Again she caught no hint of what lay behind the vivid feathers, and the woman's pulse didn't quicken.

Well, Rian had only lost five – no, ten, for Henri had been using Rian's Tears – ten Tears during the set. And it was, at least, not the fox-masked man who had won them.

The same arbiters descended, and a touch on Rian's shoulder again shifted the room about her. Another small room, a different table, and a ten-Tear drop lying between them, along with the four Tears Rian had not yet lost.

"I am very curious," the member of the Court said, mantling her wings briefly, and giving Rian a glimpse not of the red she had expected, but of milk and crystal and diamond.

"A burden you must bear," replied the arbiter, and it was Rian's own pulse that began to race.

The forfeit had clearly been pre-arranged between the two Court members. Had Rian's abilities contravened the laws of the Towers? Or was this another consequence of godly allegiance, dragging her into games where no-one explained the rules?

"Go with this one, then," the white-winged woman said, flicking fingers at the arbiter. "That is 'my' forfeit."

Rian said nothing as the ten-Tear rose from the table and vanished. Instead, she reattached her remaining four Tears to her veil, and stood. Both Court members preceded her out of the room, and the woman from the Snow Tower departed down the corridor with a flick of her pale wings.

The curve of the floor told Rian a little. It glowed with the light of the outer walls, but came the closest to horizontal that Rian had seen since she'd ascended the Gilded Tower. They must be near the central Tower, the Tower of Balance. The corridor itself was enormous: wide and tall and clear.

The arbiter, her pale hair winding around her like smoke, held out a hand and Rian, feeling childlike beside this seven-foot woman, took it as the arbiter stretched her wings. Their fragile leather membranes brought to mind rain-specked windows looking onto a city at night: dark and jewelled and glimmering.

Then the arbiter tugged Rian a little closer, turned her, and transferred her clasp to a prosaic grip under Rian's armpits. Two lazy beats sent them soaring rapidly down the corridor.

Rian, who had very recently been flying with another powerful and impressive woman, sucked in her breath and wished, suddenly, that Aerinndís Gwyn Lynn was with her. Not for protection, but simply for the wonder of it.

But Aerinndís, bound by rule to Prytennia, could not travel with Rian even if she cared to, and Rian had best put aside distraction. Whatever the purpose of this excursion, it was unlikely to be without consequences.

They were approaching a tall archway. The arbiter didn't slow, and they glided through it at what felt like a lazy pace, but was far faster than Rian would be able to walk-bounce. Beyond was an emptiness, a cup-like space circled by similar arches, and rising to a vast dome filled with shimmering twists of colour. Red, gold, blue, and milk-white. Not rainbows, but threads of liquid light.

"The Chamber of Balance."

Rian had said it aloud, and was surprised when the arbiter answered her, even as they lifted up through the bright, chilly shimmer.

"Technically, this is the antechamber. The Chamber of Balance sits above."

There was a circular structure set in the ceiling, clear to the eye only once they had passed through most of the wash of light. There were no stairs or ramps leading up to it and, rimmed by a balcony with only one doorway visible, it reminded Rian very strongly of a birdhouse.

There didn't appear to be any guards – Rian had not seen another person since firebird mask had departed – and they landed on the balcony precisely in front of the oversized doorway. Set back on her feet, Rian staggered two steps, and struggled to regain her poise. It was not just flying through low gravity that had unbalanced her. This was a place where those outside the Court of the Moon were not casually invited: the very top of the Towers of the Moon, where the Court's endless competitions were judged.

"Go in," the arbiter instructed.

'In' was another corridor, stretching left and right to follow the outer wall of the birdhouse. Rian bounce-stepped left without wasting breath on questions, and wondered if there was any significance to the choice. There were no furnishings to break up the corridor's smooth curve, but the inner wall seemed oddly textured. Punctured in patterns: a needle-fine filigree. Rian did not quite dare press her eye to the tiny holes in an attempt to see through them, but still slowed, not at all keen to know the purpose of this strange summons. On the far side of the wall, not close but within range of her senses, was a single, ponderous heartbeat.

At a point she guessed was opposite the first, she discovered another arch: this one with a door that opened as she drifted within touching distance. She stopped, steadying herself on the frame, and looked across a faintly convex floor to a chair that even at a distance of forty feet or more made her feel tiny. As did the occupant.

The Duke of Balance.

(vi)

Members of the Court of the Moon grew taller, not older. It was rare to ever see an adult that was not at least six feet tall, and seven feet was more common even for those who were seen outside the Towers. Those were the youngest generations, most likely to mix with humans. The Duke of Balance, the first of the Court to arrive in France, was among the oldest known.

If he had a name, Rian had never heard of it. None of the five Dukes who ruled the Towers were ever referred to by anything but their title. Rian did not know how tall he had been when the Court had first invaded but, so many centuries later, he was a spindly giant.

"Come."

She had barely recognised the sound as a word. His chest might look thin, but his voice was far from reedy, and the thick air of the Towers made it doubly deep.

Rian took a step forward, and then barely stopped herself from clutching the doorway again, for the floor was not there. She was looking directly down to an antlike swarm of people, far below, and the river, and the sprawling parkland that surrounded the towers, ringed by hotels and restaurants and then the streets of Lutèce, grand and small.

But directly below this room was the 'antechamber' of Balance, filled with swirling colour. The floor was not absent, or even a window, but some kind of illusion. She was not about to fall.

The irritation that followed this realisation helped, sweeping aside fear and wonder. Rian took a breath, firmed her chin, and walked forward with the light, skipping step made necessary by the low gravity. She stopped only when she could properly see the man waiting, her more than excellent night vision having no difficulty with the dim lighting of the room.

The seat of his chair would be perhaps shoulder height on Rian. The hands that curled over the armrests were... Rian blinked, but he was not clawed: his left hand was covered by a partial gauntlet of black metal. Spiked and spindly, it brought to mind the segmented legs of a crustacean. The right hand, uncovered, was neatly manicured, unremarkable barring the spider-leg length of the creamy fingers.

His clothes were similar to the close-fitted trousers and the flowing jacket that Étienne had so happily picked out earlier that day, but fashioned for a man built on pipe-cleaner lines. No veil or mask hid his face, but his dark brown hair was covered by a jewelled net of what looked to be silver and amethyst. Two thin braids studded with amethyst drops framed a long face, but the hints of purple near temple and ears were not gemstones. The stories about the older members of the Court of the Moon developing scales were apparently true.

It was difficult to judge when he was sitting down, but Rian thought him more than twice her own height. At least twelve, maybe fourteen feet tall. The back of the chair was cut to allow his wings to project past it while still providing support to his head, and even though he held them closed she could guess at a truly disconcerting span.

"I would like to see your face, please."

Rian hesitated, then lifted off the mask and veil. She glanced down at them, and noticed that a small table had appeared – grown – beside her. Feeling very exposed in her tissue-thin garments, she put the mask and veil down, and looked directly into his eyes.

"Did you arrange this? The reason that brought me to the Towers?"

"No." His deep voice, apparently kept deliberately soft, thrummed like a distant drum. "I am merely taking advantage of circumstance."

By annexing an unguarded pawn? Rian had to focus all of her wits, for she could not permit herself to be used against Prytennia. But how to extricate herself? She knew very little about the Duke of Balance: he did not ordinarily interact with outsiders to the Court of the Moon. And even most of the Court only saw him at the once-per-century adjudication of the balance of rule.

"I presume you haven't brought me here to play Forfeit."

"No." The faintest hint of a smile lightened his face. "I cannot involve myself directly in the competitions. No, I wish to propose an exchange."

"Of?"

"I wish to know a particular thing about the Amon-Re bloodline. In return..." The vibration of his voice dropped to, if possible, an even lower note. "In return, I will give you the means to gain what you seek."

Rian held herself very still. She could count on one hand the number of people who knew that the vampire who had bound her was of the Amon-Re line, instead of the Ma'at line he publicly claimed. Makepeace's real identity was something she literally could not speak of, because he had bound her against doing so. But the Duke must surely know that secret, to mention Amon-Re at all.

"The...the one who bound me has given me very little information about the bloodlines," she said, honestly enough. "I don't think I would be able to answer questions."

"Even Heriath would not be able to answer me," the Duke said, removing any doubt as to whether he knew Makepeace's real name. "Not without conducting the experiment I wish you to consent to. I want," he went on, "to know how the Amon-Re line reacts to my blood."

Rian stared. Took a long breath. Finally said: "I'm not a vampire yet."

"No. But the Amon-Re symbiont burns bright within you. There are some risks, of course. My blood would end the life of an ordinary human. You, who have survived Amon-Re, could not be killed by a drop of it, but there is a strong chance it will make you very ill. If that occurs, I will pay recompense."

But why did he want to know the effect of his blood on Amon-Re vampires? It seemed to Rian that there had to be consequences to this she could not see. And, yet, could she pass up a real chance to recover the mask? For Martine, who had done so much for Rian?

"I cannot risk allegiance," she hedged. "I am already divided."

"We are, as ever, not gods. Nothing I do could bind your allegiance to me."

"I don't...I don't know," Rian said, choosing directness in some vain hope that it would lead her to the truth. "I have become tied into the defences of my homeland. My choices are not entirely my own."

These protestations seemed to neither surprise nor concern him, and the steady pulse of his heart did not change as he said: "The consequences of this are only knowledge. The information I gain will not impact Prytennia, nor lead to any threat to that land. If you wish for fuller disclosure, the eventual goal of this experiment will greatly impact Aquitania, if I am able to progress to it."

Aquitania, the southern province of France, was highly disputed territory. It should not surprise Rian at all that the Dukes were looking for ways to retain it permanently. But how could Rian tasting this ancient creature's blood alter that? And what would the various powers she was tied to think of her becoming involved?

"What goal?"

"That, at the moment, is not relevant, since I cannot progress toward that until you are more who you will be."

She didn't fully understand the sentence. "More what?"

The soft rumble of a voice seemed to echo from the whole of the shadowy, circular room. "You are a power in the process of becoming. You have weight, and the world bends itself around you. When you have taken more steps along that path, you will have the strength for a further exchange. But that is a bargain for another century."

Rian usually prided herself on her quick thinking, but she was struggling to process all this. Next century? She would almost certainly be a vampire in truth by then. Remarkable to think of even being alive. Did he seriously plan on her returning here in a century...to drink his blood?

She needed clarity. There had been too many bargains these last few months, and each time they had twisted into something larger. Contracting for ten years of service with a vampire had become an irreversible step toward vampirism. Giving allegiance to the god Cernunnos had brought her a nice house and salary – and put her square in the centre of political and godly battles. No matter what terms the Duke of Balance offered, it would be stupid not to expect a significant consequence.

She did not need to do this. She could simply walk away. And watch Martine lose the position she had fought so hard to gain, and which had finally allowed her to hold her head high, lifting her above the 'shame' of Milo's birth.

Rian stood still for a long time, watched by the winged giant, and listening to the steady pulse, pulse, pulse of his blood. Then she carefully restated what he had asked, to be sure, and added: "If your experiment is successful, there is another stage that you wish to move on to, next century, which will have consequences for Aquitania. Does that stage require me as well?"

"Not specifically. But Amon-Re vampires are very rare."

Amon-Re vampires could be counted on one hand, because their blood killed almost all who aspired to ascend to their powers. That gave Rian an advantage.

"There is a shortfall in your calculation," she said carefully. "Why do you think that I will return to France next century?"

"Have you not returned to it again and again?" he asked, without any hint of concern.

"I have family I love here, and France is filled with things I appreciate and enjoy. But by next century all the people I care about in Lutèce will be gone. And without them, for all its delights, France is not a place that welcomes me. If I married here, all my property would become my husband's. If I attended the Gilded Court's games without a mask, I would become an object of disdain. I came here tonight with a cousin in part because a woman travelling alone, dressed like this, could be seen as forfeiting a right to protest any form of mistreatment."

"Those are not the mores of the Court of the Moon."

"No. In fact, it's probably the Roman influence on Aquitania, mixing north," Rian said. "Before the formation of Prytennia, there were similar attitudes all over Albion, but when Sulis Answered, her laws became the country's laws. In France you, who claim not to be gods, do not care about human laws because only the Court's rules are important to your battles – and those rules change four times a century, and only matter at night."

A sliding movement behind the Duke was his only immediate response. His wings, glimmering night, slowly expanded, stretching to almost the full diameter of the room. Rian, watching mesmerised, felt as if she were wearing the mask of a mouse, not a snake.

Then he said: "Are you asking me to dictate to the Sun Court?"

Spoken as calmly as the rest of their discussion, but the question practically clanged warnings. Rian had not missed that the Duke of Balance appeared to be attempting to live up to his name in trying to arrange his experiments. What price could she possibly pay equal to telling the Sun Court to alter the common laws of France?

But Rian was not quite so young and foolish as to ask the Duke of Balance for anything at all, let alone a thing so potentially large. And she was not a mouse.

If she truly was a power in the process of becoming, she would test her weight.

"I am telling you that the laws of the Sun Court pronounce me 'less than', and actively hurt people I care about. They are..." She paused. "I think they are one of the reasons I have never made France my home. And they are now an obstacle standing in the way of your plans for Aquitania."

There was no need to make the point clearer. He was not stupid. He wanted something from her – a small thing tonight and a very large thing on another night, a century from now. To even ask, to begin to negotiate for whatever it was he wanted from the vampire she would be, this pipe-cleaner giant needed her to come to him.

His outstretched wings stirred, and her tissue-dress shifted in response. But he did not even seem to be looking at her, was gazing a little to her left toward the floor, as if he was watching the images of the city. She noticed that the great river of his bloodstream was flowing at a faster rate, but she did not believe this to be anger, or a prelude to any attack. Still, she could not restrain a tiny sigh of relief when that mantle of star-studded night folded away, and he looked back at her as calmly as ever.

"You may find that your errand tonight leads to a small choice with large consequences," he said. "I will leave to you whether the result is enough to encourage your return during the new century. Do I have your agreement for this first experiment?"

"Yes."

He inclined his head the tiniest degree. Gratitude from a not-a-god to someone who was not a power yet. His gaze shifted to his left hand, shielded by the partial gauntlet, as he pierced the pad of his own thumb with one of the spikes. Then he rested his hand palm-up on his knee, so that the rapidly welling drop of blood was just within Rian's reach.

Rian might have been bitten by a vampire, but she had no taste for blood – beyond some very uncomfortable memories of the complications of the Amon-Re ability to sense emotion. It was necessary to steel herself, to remind herself of Martine, before she could move closer to him. That gauntlet of curving metal claws only emphasised the sense that she was walking into a snare. It would be like putting her face into a bear-trap.

She would have to stand on tip-toe to do it, as well. Made even smaller by proximity, she said: "This is *not* what I expected to be doing tonight," and heard a rumble-puff of laughter as she licked his thumb.

An iron tang filled her mouth. She swallowed, relieved the stuff didn't burn as Makepeace's did.

The floor tilted.

(vii)

Drunk in the street, and weeping. Ashamed by the hurt wine failed to drown, by the fool she had been. Martine, an arm around her waist, guiding her back to the hotel, and reminding her that she was alive, and survival was a victory when your lover had tried to have you erased.

Memory receded, divided, and a scarlet thread led Rian back to that street in Lutèce, long ago.

Clinging to a lamp post, shouting at Martine. Words born of hurt, cruel sneers. Martine's white face, marked by the red outline of a hand. A disjointed maze of shadowed streets. A step behind her, a blow. Then...chiming. The high voices of la clochettes, and she among them, in the Court of the Moon's Otherworld.

She had always known Martine had saved her life that night. Struggling to separate herself from a memory of something that had never been, Rian tried to orient herself among a maze of ribbons and threads. Vivid, dull, faded, brilliant. They pulled at her, and she fell down the nearest, glittering and strawberry-ripe.

Floating in a forest of shivering trees. Hide-and-seek, one of dozens in gowns of silk and nothing. A woman with dark hair, a swan's face, and wings of ice shared a conspiratorial glance with Rian as they dodged the eyes of hunters.

A game of Forfeit? Rian shook herself free and immediately lost herself to a plum-dark thread.

Hands dragged her down, while the winds hauled her up, and Rian cried out, torn between death and the Night Breezes. And then Aerinndís Gwyn Lynn was there, lifting her free, and for a moment Rian had her arms wrapped...

The thread twisted, split.

Rian cried out, torn between death and the Night Breezes. A bone parted, and she screamed. The Night Breezes scattered...

A thick scarlet shimmer caught her.

She stood on tip-toe, bare feet planted on one of his thighs, and bit delicately into his long throat.

A glimpse only, before a mulberry thread caught her.

Lying at his feet in a pool of her own waste and vomit, wondering what Martine would do now.

Rian squeezed her eyes shut, blocking ribbons and threads. She *was* on the floor, but not ill. And she clutched...not a lamp post. The rhythmic pulse of his blood steadied her. She listened to it, ear pressed to cloth, until most of the dizziness had gone, and then she risked opening her eyes.

The ribbons and threads were all still there, but less dominant, and they no longer dragged her into them. This, then, was the power of the Tower of Balance. She had not known that their ability to 'follow the lines of consequence' meant they could see possible pasts as well.

Should she be glad she hadn't seen anything of import? Only confirmation of her probable return, in a century's time, to bite him. And that she'd had her hair cut short, and was not so terribly dressed, the next time.

That was useful to know, but she had to focus on the current century. One hand at a time, she let go of the Duke of Balance's leg.

"How long have I been sitting like this?"

A thrumming told her: "A little under an hour."

She looked up, finding it uncommonly dark, but it was only when he shifted them that she realised that he'd had his wings folded forward and around them both. Their movement was like the night sky tidying itself away.

"Do you see the world like that all the time?"

"When I exert myself. I wished to know how much you could endure."

Her current view was of leg and leg. So much leg. Rian stood, taking stock of herself. The straps of the tissue dress were askew, and she'd lost one of her soft dancing shoes, but she did not feel ill, and the dizziness was almost entirely gone.

"And now you know," she said, finding her shoe. "Do you consider it a successful experiment?"

"Yes."

She felt more than heard the word. Rian's ability to sense emotion rarely worked with beings of considerable power, but she was suddenly sure that this mattered to the Duke of Balance. Not because he had taken a step toward bringing some complex scheme to fruition, but on a deeply emotional level. She took a step away from him, but only so she could properly see his face. This was inscrutable, but she had expected nothing else.

"Well, since I don't know what you hope to gain by having the person I'll be drink from you, I won't wish you luck. But I hope circumstances arrange themselves to the point where you can tell me."

"Thank you," he said, simply. "Alexandrine will take you to the halls."

Accepting dismissal, Rian offered him a sketch of a curtsey, and collected her mask and veil. This last was heavy, and she counted ten night-dark teardrops hanging from its edge. She put it on without comment, settled her mask in place, and left.

(viii)

The Court member with champagne-coloured hair was sitting on the edge of the circular outer balcony, dangling her legs over the enormous chamber of coloured light. A single red thread and two ribbons phased into Rian's view above the woman, but Rian resisted any impulse to try to follow them.

"Is your name Alexandrine?"

The woman glanced up at her, and nodded.

"Mine's Rian. Do you ever find it difficult not to talk about all the things you see and hear during the competitions of the Court?"

"Not at all," Alexandrine said. "Most of it is very dull. The interesting matters are those that it would be sheer stupidity to discuss." She stood up, still more than a foot taller than Rian, but no longer seeming so formidable.

"Do you ever wish you could participate?"

Alexandrine's smooth features twisted with lively amusement. "For every thing I might envy, there are ten I am glad to avoid. Fashion, for instance."

Rian laughed, and allowed herself be picked up by the armpits once again. But instead of launching into the shifting light below, they changed location with abrupt, unsettling immediacy, to an alcove in a curving corridor.

The slope told Rian they'd left the area around the Tower of Balance, and she was not surprised when a few lazy beats of Alexandrine's wings brought them to the entrance of a completely different open room. The upper assembly hall of the Gilded Tower.

Rian's first impression was of space and music. The place was enormous – larger even than the antechamber of the Hall of Balance – and even an orchestra should have been swallowed up by it, but instead sound filled the entrance where Rian and Alexandrine stood. Delicate, fluting melody, but with an underlying beat.

Like the hall on the lower tier, the room sat at a conjunction in the curving filigree of the dome, and sloped grandly. One side rose in tiers, while the curving ceiling also provided a far wall, and was studded with wide balconies. The flattest area rested in between these two points, like a stage within a particularly vertical amphitheatre. Rian could not track the number of people – the vast majority winged – walking and flitting and dancing. One thousand? Two? And every one of them complicated by a halo of ribbons and threads.

"The Dukes," Alexandrine said, indicating the balconies. "And the Sun Court."

The five largest balconies, best positioned to watch the wide central part of the room, stood out for the height of most of the occupants. Four Dukes, for the four ruling towers, each as attenuated as the Duke of Balance. Around their great chairs stood figures that were small only by comparison.

The fifth balcony belonged to a collection of miniatures. No wings, no long spindly limbs. The Sun Court. A dozen humans, all of them veiled and masked, but doubtless the five seated would be the Royal Family. Even the Dauphin's young son was present – presumably for a ceremonial appearance, since the revels of the Gilded Tower hardly seemed suitable for a boy of eight.

Rian's attention, however, was for the woman seated on the opposite side of the King from the Dauphin, Dauphine and their son. The Dauphin's older child, Princess Heloise. And, though it was impossible to be certain at this distance whether it was the correct mask, standing behind her chair was a slim man wearing the face of a lion.

"Midnight approaches, and with it the night's primary challenge," Alexandrine said. "The rules are beneath the Time of Red Petals."

This seemed to be an enormous arrangement of flowers, not too far to Rian's left.

"What–?" Rian began, but Alexandrine was gone. Rian had been 'given the means' and now she, somehow, had to work out how to take advantage of the opportunity.

The thick scent of roses swamped Rian's senses as she approached 'the Time of Red Petals' and found a clock the size of a cartwheel. Twenty minutes before midnight. Immediately below the clock's face, an elaborately curlicued notice set out the rules of an elaborate three-stage challenge.

A hunt. A hunt combined with hide-and-seek. It would cost potentially all of Rian's Tears of the Night to play, put already-inadequate clothing at risk, and the winner would walk away with, according to the notice, 'A Pool of Tears'. A fortune dazzling enough to momentarily steal Rian's breath.

Forfeit is a game you play to lose.

Étienne would appreciate all this enormously, and in other circumstances Rian supposed she might find herself stimulated. But the need to win the Mask of Léon overshadowed every distraction. How? There was no obvious path to the viewing platform where the royal family were located. Would D'Argent enter the challenge? And what did the rules mean by "participants will be determined by song's touch"?

Rather than dither, Rian found the nearest convenience and tidied herself, and then collected a small plate from one of the many tables of refreshments. Sitting down, she ate and looked for solutions.

Music. Dancers, effortless and graceful in the sweeping movements dictated by low gravity. A swirl of la clochettes.

A few feet away from Rian three red-winged women faced a taller blue-winged woman.

One of the threads around the taller woman tugged at Rian, and she cautiously followed it, wary of ending up on the floor again. But – perhaps because it was not her own thread – she was not thrust so completely into experiencing 'a possibility', but saw it more as an image. The blue-winged woman, sword in hand, held the red-wings at bay.

That was most likely a challenge during the reign of the Tower of the Drum. Swords were not at all easy weapons to use in low gravity, but there was a long tradition of using them during the Drum's reign. Rian was not quite close enough to hear whatever the leader of the red-winged women was saying, but all four departed together.

A few minutes of experimentation showed Rian she could not follow every thread or ribbon of those in her view, but only those that tugged at her when she concentrated on them. Distance did not seem to limit this ability, so she turned her attention hopefully back to the Sun Court's balcony.

Although the man in the lion mask had a generous swathe of ribbons attached to him, none of them tugged at Rian. Perhaps it was too far. She tried the Princess instead, and then the King, but nothing happened. Frustrated, Rian let out her breath and watched, hoping for clues to reaching the balcony, as the Dauphin and Dauphine rose and collected their young son, ushering him toward a rear door.

A ribbon attached to the boy tugged at Rian, and she followed it and saw him *a few years older, shouting angrily, then breaking off to scratch at two stretched red lumps above his shoulder-blades. Wings, in their first stage of visible development.*

Rian blinked away from the image, and stared at the small family. The boy was a chrysalide: a child born to one of the Court of the Moon and a human woman. And thus not the Dauphin's son, and not heir to France after his supposed father.

Did all the members of the Tower of Balance know this? Was this the 'means' Rian had been given to regain the Mask of Léon? Princess Heloise would certainly...what?

Heloise had been the Dauphin's only child until she was fourteen. The birth of her brother had meant that instead of eventually ruling beside a carefully chosen husband, she would be a tool to strengthen alliances. Common wisdom expected a marriage to Prince Gustav of Sweden within the year.

Rian, who had met Gustav and liked him, and would never ever want to be married to him, did not know enough about Heloise to guess whether she would find his energy – and collection of mistresses – at all tolerable. The princess had been a noted participant in the salons during the Sky Tower's reign, when the Arts were celebrated above all else. She was also a patron of the theatres, but her reputation, balanced between honouring the Court of the Moon and matching the multiple intersecting definitions of a 'proper' woman in France, kept her generally circumspect. The friends known as her myrmidons were at least not openly her lovers.

What would D'Argent do with information about the young prince, if Rian tried to use it to trade for the mask? Should Rian attempt to approach the princess instead?

Was this her small choice with large consequences?

Setting the question aside, Rian looked about her until she spotted an arbiter, and went to ask what 'determined by song's touch' meant.

"Chosen by the sweet-singers," the man said, rather unhelpfully, and then added: "Listen. You can hear them."

The fluting music had died away, to be replaced by a single pure tone. Thin at first, but swelling into a knife that cut through the breastbone and exposed something quivering. At the point where it became painful, the sound transformed into a chorus, an exchange of notes, and then they came, flooding up from the sloping curve beneath the balconies. Tiny motes in shades of soft fawn and dark brown, moving as a cloud but then dispersing and settling toward the room's revellers.

Rian had expected birds, and so it was not until one of the motes dropped onto her head, and then scuttled down her arm, that she saw that the sweet-singers were tiny furry animals – similar in design to squirrels, except with a stretch of skin between front and back limbs. Not-quite wings. The one that had landed on Rian was smaller than her hand, but with twice as much plumy dark tail, currently wrapped around her wrist.

"There," said the arbiter, faintly amused. "You have been chosen."

"I've never heard of them before," Rian said, lifting her hand to better study the tiny creature. Primarily pale faun, with stripes of chocolatey brown edging to black across eyes, cheeks and neck, and then down the spine. Another shot past, not using its wings for flight, but instead vibrating its tail.

"It is rare for them to come to the Towers," the arbiter said.

Rian wondered whether the sweet-singers, like other inhabitants of the Court's Otherworld, were reborn human souls but, before she could ask, a murmur of interest rose and the arbiter turned, watching gravely. Rian followed the line of his gaze and saw that several of the tiny motes had zipped up to the level of the balconies.

"The current leaders of the challenges, the season's champions, stand with the Dukes," the arbiter told her.

But attention was not for the four largest balconies. Instead, the crowd – or at least the humans among it – watched King Florentin, and beside him his granddaughter, directly in the path of one tiny, swiftly-moving creature.

The air of anticipation in the room was palpable. The Sun Court's princess might dress herself in impractical clothing and sit to watch the Gilded Court's revels, but participating, even behind the 'feather's breadth of deniability' of the masks, would be the height of poor judgment. There was an enormous gap between 'believed to be doing' and 'seen to be doing'.

Did the princess have the option to *not* enter the challenge? Would it offend the Court of the Moon if she refused, or would she pay the price of her reputation for not leaving the room before midnight? She at least made no move to leap from her chair and dodge for the nearest exit, watching the approaching flyer as calmly as the Duke of Balance.

The man in the lion mask stepped in front of her, and Rian was as pleased as the crowd disappointed. This development put D'Argent within Rian's reach, and at least suggested something of his personality.

Raising the hand decorated by sweet-singer in front of him, D'Argent bowed his head to it, and then more deeply to the King and Princess Heloise, before turning and leaping precipitately off the balcony to the crowds below, the long skirts of his coat billowing.

The sweet-singer riding Rian's own hand piped two ascending notes, so pure and piercing that Rian shivered.

"Assemble with the chosen," the arbiter instructed. "You are to dance the song of the sweet-singers before each stage of the challenge."

"They're calling the tune now, are they?" Rian murmured, considering the tiny creature firmly attached to her wrist. It watched her alertly in return. "And who pulls *your* strings?" Rian added in an undertone, then shrugged and joined the crowd.

(ix)

Five hundred chosen. Rian knew the number because one of the members of the Gilded Tower playing organiser was counting half under her breath as the dancers were gently prodded into groups sorted by height. Toward the very centre of the crowd they rose to nine and ten feet tall, but at least a third of the dancers were human, and most of the Court members were in the seven-foot range.

Rian, unsurprisingly, found herself matched with other humans, and a single shorter Court member: barely six feet tall. The Court member, a woman with vividly blue wings wearing a peacock mask, gave them a centre for a well-known opening formation.

The Dance of Fives, as old as the Towers. The symbolism was obvious, and the woman of the Sky Tower seemed to relish situating herself as the Tower of Balance. Rian and the three others in the group placed their right hands on her shoulder, and waited as the last dancers shuffled into place. The whole room – audience, organisers, dancers – fell silent.

Song, the sweet-singers, pierced the air.

With a less familiar measure, Rian may have stumbled, but the Dance of Fives was something every child in France learned, and every visitor who wanted to dance beneath the Towers was taught. She moved automatically, and kept her step when wings flared in the groups around them. Even when her group's centre dancer, lifted ceremoniously in the air, stretched her wings to their fullest and spun before dropping down, Rian kept dancing, breathing in time with the pure and perfectly synchronised piping of the sweet-singers.

It had the air of ritual. This was how the Dance of Fives was meant to be. The sweet-singers, the glimmer and flare of wings, the swirling leaps. Rian was mesmerised. Exhilarated. And, for the first time that night, aware of those around her as more than obstacles in the way of her goal. When peacock-mask swirled down, each layer of her fountain dress separated, and Rian watched, and felt the woman's pleasure, and thought about the forfeits she might pay – or take. If Aerinndís were here...no, Rian did not want to court Aerinndís in a milieu such as this. But she very much wanted to dance with her.

The song ended, and Rian reminded herself of the one forfeit that was important that night. She looked around for a lion.

A single turn discovered a kingly half-mask almost directly behind her, close enough that the wearer might have heard her indrawn breath if excited murmurs had not risen to fill the space left empty by song. The crowd was already moving, and Rian shifted a little closer, studying worn leather, tracing tiny lines in the cracked silver paint. The Mask of Léon, without a doubt, worn by a man of middle height who looked young and fit and was presumably an actor calling himself Lionel D'Argent.

Had he taken the mask because of his name, or because he recognised it as the original? Would there be consequences even if she made him give it up?

Rian followed D'Argent silently, weighing up her chances of winning one of his ten-Tears during the challenge, and whether she needed to aim for two. If she failed to gain any, then she would need to find a chance to talk to him, and bargain. Given the busy pace of the challenge, there would be few opportunities.

The gold-winged organisers ushered the crowd inward, past what must be the main entrance to the hall, and beyond the vast broad shaft of the Gilded Tower. So they would play in the flatter central reaches, not the near-vertical outer edges of the dome? Good. Wingless humans were already at enough of a disadvantage.

Rian's sweet-singer, chirruping softly, clambered up to her shoulder and tugged deftly at her veil. A single inky ten-Tear came away, and the sweet-singer pressed it to its stomach before launching itself into the growing cloud of similarly burdened fellows.

Rian looked away, and found herself in a forest. She blinked at spindly white trees growing directly from the floor – and walls and ceiling – of the corridor she had been funnelled toward. The trees were the same glowing white as the walls, and could well be elaborate sculpture, though so delicate they trembled and swayed with every breath or movement.   The Towers and domes grew like living creatures, so perhaps these pale trees lived as well.

"Find the song, avoid the hunters!" the organisers were calling, and others around Rian were not slow to move – some shooting into the air, and others bounce-walking rapidly forward – and then checking when it became clear that there were few open spaces in this sky forest.

One of the flyers, though, made a pleased noise even as she banked and hovered, plucking from the trembling white leaves a long, dark droplet.   The woman held it up to consider the image it held, that of the person the ten-Tear belonged to, and then attached it to her veil.

A single, distant note caught Rian's attention.   Her sweet-singer, waiting at a gathering point.   Rian had to reach her sweet-singer within the time limit or pay a penalty.   She also had to give up a ten-Tear to gain entry to the first gathering place, and would rather it wasn't another of her own.

This part of the sky forest filled a maze of curling filigree tunnels, with Rian's path constantly detouring through side-corridors.   The Tears of the Night at least stood out clearly against the pale leaves and branches, and Rian found her first ten-Tear without any difficulty at all.   She held it up, and saw a spindly man with red wings, wearing a Yue dragon mask.   One of five hundred ten-Tears, and she would need a fine serving of luck to find D'Argent's.

Spotting another ten-Tear high above, Rian hesitated. She could not reach that with a bound, and would need to pull herself up – not difficult in the gravity, but noisy.

A low growling, far behind, served to remind Rian of some of the obstacles in this hunt, and she decided to move quickly toward the call of her sweet-singer, missing an opportunity for another ten-Tear when a woman in a swan mask reached it first.

The woman then hastily stepped behind a tree and held herself as still as possible, and though she was far from hidden, the ruse was apparently sufficient to avoid the gargouille that galumphed directly past and captured Rian instead.

It did this with all the grinning enthusiasm fifteen feet of snake-dog could muster, coiling around her in an excess of triumph, and Rian could not help but give its flat-snouted head a pat, even as two of the la clochettes who had been riding it dove with a distinctly mocking cascade of sound, and lifted away one of the layers of Rian's fountain dress as penalty.

They'd taken the under-layer, which was a clever trick indeed, and left Rian in a knee-high dress. The loss at least allowed Rian to concentrate on speed and searching, since the rules allowed only one capture by hunters in each of the three segments of the challenge.

The deep note of a gong warned her that the three-quarter mark had passed, and she decided to move on, searching for the meeting point. Even though the sky forest was full of seekers, Rian could hear only the song of her own sweet-singer above the rattle of disturbed leaves. It was fortunately close. Yes, there to the right the trees opened up. Not to a space large enough to hold five hundred, but still a solid crowd.

Rian was stopped by a pair of members of the Gilded Tower, and handed over dragon mask's ten-Tear as payment for passing the stage before the gong sounded a second time. This, along with any ten-Tears not discovered among the leaves, would go to make up the challenge's prize.

One ten-Tear down, with two increasingly expensive stages to go, Rian briefly entertained the shining vision of winning that bounty, but knew her chances were minimal. She had, thankfully, enough to complete the entire challenge without risking Tears of the Sun, and only felt a faint pang at spending them. The Tears of the Night did not represent her own money, though she was still not entirely certain how much she had paid the Duke of Balance for them.

Her sweet-singer landed lightly on her shoulder, tiny claws pricking bare skin. It piped, as if in greeting, and she stroked its head delicately, wondering why she was so sure it was the same one.

The piping multiplied, as other sweet-singers returned to their chosen, and their voices merged into another recognisable tune. The players responded: finding partners, linking hands. Rian found two members of the Court, and placed her right hand on top of theirs, sharing their faint laughter at how far up she had to reach. Then they danced.

A spiral of three, a pattern of nine, of twenty-seven, of seventy-one, all in a slow circular promenade. Dancers were exchanged from group to group, clasping hands and considering each other, deciding whose ten-Tears they hoped to capture.

Rian could feel marked interest among those whose hands she briefly clasped, and also the general growing anticipation of the crowd. She saw D'Argent and watched him moving, swift and elegant, but the exchanges gave her no chance to talk or dance with him, and the next stage of the challenge began immediately after the end of the song, with each sweet-singer flitting off with two ten-Tears.

The crowd followed into twilight, for the walls, ceiling, floor and forest beyond the clearing lacked the full-moon brilliance of the areas already passed, blurring detail without truly confusing the path.

The vague shadows were easy enough for a not-quite-vampire to navigate, and Rian found her first ten-Tear almost immediately. She held it up to consider a human woman in a tiger mask. Attaching the Tear to her veil, she moved on quickly, shivering a little, for the sky forest seemed to have developed a cool mist.

With the chill came a hush, muffling even the rattle of disturbed leaves, and   seeming to add distance to the sweet-singer. And there was more scent, sharp notes of pine and loam...

Rian stopped short. There was dirt underneath her soft slippers. Stars above. Wind touched her. These were not things of the Towers of the Moon, of the strange sky forest that grew but perhaps did not live. This was the Great Forest, the world-spanning Otherworld tied by vows of allegiance to her soul.

And she was hunted.

Rian did not question that certainty, immediately abandoning her search for ten-Tears and concentrating on finding her way out. This was part of the price she paid for her allegiance to Cernunnos: the Horned King was hunter and hunted. But it was the forest itself that judged and tested her, and she did not care to learn what failure would mean.

There were no paths. Behind spread the silence that came to forests when tooth and claw moved with purpose. Rian, in three layers of nothing much, and slippers that let her feel every stone, did not run. Her only hope was to move as quietly and smoothly as possible, to try to keep ahead of what stalked her so that it could not properly discover her location.

The sweet-singer's call pulled at her, and Rian struggled to maintain a smooth pace, watching her feet and doing her best to avoid fallen twigs and dry leaves. She did not run: she danced a secret course along twisting tree roots, skipped to stone, to dirt, to the gnarled skirts of another wooden partner. She did not run.

She. Did. Not. Run.

The call of the sweet-singer swelled, piercing, encouraging. A twig snapped behind her. Close! So close! Rian bit her lip, but did not break the dance, did not rush, not even when she saw the edge of a clearing ahead of her. She kept her pace, stepped lightly, and emerged.

(x)

A clearing in the sky forest, large enough for five hundred chosen. Rian was obviously on the trailing edge, arriving past the time limit, though she had not heard the gong. A cluster of la clochettes whirled around her in a cascade of sound, and when they departed she wore a hip-length dress.

Rian was past caring. She paid over the cost of completing the stage, saw there were places to sit and things to drink, and took a glass before sinking thankfully into the nearest chair. Her feet throbbed, though the bruises were already hurting less. That was the vampiric symbiont, hard at work.

Her sweet-singer found her almost immediately, and nestled against her throat, tail curled around her neck. It took much longer for Rian to spot the silver lion among the crowd, but eventually the sweep of the dance brought D'Argent into view. He'd lost his coat, but otherwise seemed in fine fettle as he was passed between partners.

It was a dance of pairs, and an opportunity that might not come again, so Rian climbed to reluctant feet and was ready for the next exchange.

D'Argent murmured politely as she stepped into the flow of the dance, and regarded her with a straightforward attraction, combined with deep wariness.

"You have been watching me, Mademoiselle Serpent."

An observant man, then. "Yes," she agreed, simply.

"Perhaps I have something on my face?"

Rian laughed. "You do. I was wondering if you would bargain for it."

His mild surprise came through to her clearly, then curiosity and a thread of anger. She wondered if she'd ever met him, for she knew many French actors. He did not *feel* familiar, and mask and veil together made it extremely difficult discern his face. Dark eyes, behind the mask.

"You recognise it, then? A thing out of place. Are you, then, a friend of a faded star?"

This wasn't good. He'd recognised not only the mask, but the one he'd won it from.

"No," she said, not allowing herself to examine how disastrous such knowledge could be to Martine. "In this matter, I am a friend of things being returned to their right and proper place."

"But me, I like it where it is." He was entertained, but not particularly sympathetic. "Try to win it, if you will." He glanced down at her two tissue layers. "I think you will not succeed."

The sweet-singers brought dance and conversation to an end, reaching forward to take three ten-Tears from their veils. Rian watched D'Argent's fly into the forest, since that would at least give her a starting direction.

"I think I will talk to you later, Monsieur," she said, and set out into a forest quite as large as the Gilded Tower's assembly hall, but barely lit: the blackness relieved only by the glimmering of countless leaves, and by dim, occasional points of light on floor, walls and ceiling. In the bare gravity of the tower, it was like swimming into the stars.

Despite their dark colour, the Tears of the Night stood out particularly well among the motes, glowing with a purple radiance that transformed them into small moons. Able to see the branches and trunks tolerably well thanks to her symbiont, Rian skipped toward the nearest moon, but changed direction as several partially-clad figures also converged. Here on the fringes there would be too much competition: best to try to push ahead.

The path she followed seemed to be sloping upward, and she realised that there were wide, spiralling ramps in the forest, allowing the wingless to access the upper reaches, and ensuring the centre of the sprawling chamber was not left empty. Rian bounced quickly forward until she was at least a third of the way into this part of the forest, and then she slowed, oriented on the nearest luminous purple bauble, and headed toward it.

After barely a glance at the image of a mouse-masked owner, Rian attached the ten-Tear to her veil. This round was her chance to regain some losses, for her night vision gave her an immense advantage, allowing her to move through the sky forest at relative speed – and forewarning her of this round's hunters.

Three lithe shapes were moving down the slope ahead. They resembled stoats or weasels, but banded black and white, and as long as Rian was tall. Each was ridden by one of the la clochettes, but the tiny sprites were silent, clutching the ears of the furred hunters, straining to see through the glimmering dark.

Any movement risked drawing their attention, so Rian stood her ground. But she could not hide her scent, and the three coursed toward her...then shied away, flinching almost, and disappearing over the side of the broad, curving slope.

Rian stood in the Great Forest, in the sky forest, in a place of night and shivering leaves. Around her slid long bodies: not of the gargouille, or the striped weasels, but of the golden-horned amasen of Cernunnos, the great snakes of good fortune. She no longer wore the mask of the snake, but of the stag, and she strode unimpeded, all barriers falling from her path as she took into her hands droplets of night. Bear. Dove. Silver lion.

The stag mask vanished when Rian took up D'Argent's ten-Tear. Panting faintly, she looked about and saw she had been brought to the brink of a pool of light spilling through a vast doorway. That had been a new experience. Cernunnos himself had walked with her. Were the night's events his doing, after all? Or was he simply lending his power because of the bond of allegiance between them, and because the challenge triggered his own circumstances? The hunter became the hunted. The hunted, in turn, would hunt.

She had arrived well ahead of the pack, and paid over a mouse and a bear and a dove to complete the round, then passed through the doorway into a sumptuously appointed star-shaped hall.

Among the provisions for comfort and further gaming were a generous scattering of members of the Tower of Balance, ready to oversee the payment of forfeits, and Rian was not in the least surprised to find Alexandrine standing at her elbow. Cernunnos was not the only power pulling her strings this night, whether the Duke of Balance called himself a god or not.

"Are these games always so elaborate?" she asked Alexandrine.

"This is one of the major challenges," Alexandrine said. "To honour the sweet-singers."

"It's something they enjoy?" Her sweet-singer had not wafted down to join her, though she could still make out its voice, clear in the growing chorus above.

"In a manner, they are competing as you have done. As if with a race of horses."

The black-winged woman looked amused, but did not outright suggest Rian represented a poorly-chosen outlier at long odds. As was to be expected with any wild gamble, Rian had not performed well. She had achieved her primary goal, but the game had cost her eight of her own ten-Tears, which ironically – or as a matter of suspicious coincidence – left her with Tears equal to the cost she had paid for double entry to the Towers in the first place. And one more.

"I have a forfeit I would like to claim," she told Alexandrine, raising D'Argent's ten-Tear. "Whenever that is possible."

Entirely unsurprised, Alexandrine nodded, and touched Rian's shoulder. The world shifted, and Rian found herself alone in a room where shimmering curtains wavered in not-very-vertical directions, as if they were reaching out to the single table and two chairs set in the room's centre.

Rian sat down, and briefly inspected her feet. The bruises no longer hurt, though small purple circles marked where she'd found particularly sharp stones or gnarled roots. She wondered if she'd get the rest of her dress back, when all of this was done. The rules hadn't been clear on that point, and it would be awkward travelling even the short distance to the special Towers train in only two layers of gossamer shimmer.

"I compliment you, Mademoiselle."

Rian glanced up from contemplation of her clothing, and found that Alexandrine had returned with D'Argent – who thankfully still wore the Mask of Léon. At last. Time to finish this.

(xi)

From the count of the ten-Tears hanging from his veil, D'Argent had been a little more successful in the challenge than Rian, but her last fear – that he had obtained one of her ten-Tears, and thus could cancel out her forfeit through exchange – was quickly assuaged, and so she said briskly:

"My forfeit is the custody of the mask of a silver lion."

Alexandrine nodded briefly, and D'Argent's ten-Tear rose from the table, and split into two fragments, one of which vanished. The man promptly unlaced his mask and handed it to Rian.

"Thank you," she said, interested to see that the ribbons and threads that surrounded him so thickly had shifted when he gave up the mask. Some had grown more prominent, and others had receded.

With the veil concealing only his lower face, D'Argent was revealed to be quite a young man, with fine black eyes, lightly-marked brows, and dark brown hair.

"I look forward to seeing it again," he said, with emphasis.

That was, at the very least, a promise to check to see that she returned it to the Sourné. Rian put the mask on the table, and glanced at the remainder of his ten-Tear, worried he would pursue the question of how the Mask of Léon had fallen into Henri's hands.

"Do you wish to claim another forfeit?" Alexandrine asked, obligingly.

Rian hesitated, for she had been left with only a small number of D'Argent's Tears. How would he react if she attempted to extract a binding promise from him, but failed because she did not have enough for the cost?

And what to do about her discoveries regarding the Prince Royal?

"Is it so very hard to decide?" D'Argent asked, sounding amused. Still standing, he leaned forward in order to gaze into her eyes through her mask. "I do not think I have ever met you before."

"It seems very unlikely," Rian said, blinking at the complex array of emotions that near proximity revealed. Genuine entertainment, a note of desire, but also a distinct sense of pride, and of challenge.

"Are you, perhaps, thinking of constraining me in some way, Mademoiselle Serpent?" he murmured.

Threat. Excitement. Determination. Even if she had sufficient Tears to extract a binding promise, Rian would not pursue it with this one. He would most certainly seek a way around the terms of whatever she asked, and exact revenge for her effrontery. But she was now sure he wouldn't let the matter drop, even if she didn't push him to retaliation.

Wanting a little more time, Rian said: "No need to loom over me. Why not sit down, so we can talk?"

D'Argent snorted, but moved to obey, and Rian took the opportunity to focus on the threads and ribbons wavering around him, making another attempt to delve into them. This time she was rewarded.

D'Argent, face unveiled and alight with a kind of savage pleasure, leaned out from the engine of an elderly steam train and shot at an autocarriage crowded with people. He handed his empty pistol to a woman with short-cropped hair – perhaps a sister, from the strong resemblance – and took from her a loaded replacement.

Interesting, but not useful. As D'Argent sat down, Rian tried again.

Gustav of Sweden: big, blond and grand in furs, at the centre of a crowded hall. He faced a woman whose long brown hair was unbound, restrained only by one of the elaborate Swedish marriage crowns. Ceremoniously, he offered her a sword with a golden armlet balanced on the hilt. No joy or dissatisfaction disturbed an expression of perfect neutrality. Her dark eyes were steady.

Rian blinked away the scene and looked across at the person now settled in the chair opposite. No stranger to the art of cosmetics, she mentally darkened brows and lashes, and made comparisons to two very different visions.

Heloise. This was Princess Heloise.

Rian had met women who dressed as men to escape walls that kept them small, and she'd also known people who used clothing to express a true reflection of their heart. Either could be true for Heloise, and it helped Rian not at all in taking her next step. She had been given a clear illustration of two very different futures for the princess, but did not even know which choice would lead to which outcome. Or how much the Duke of Balance had guided what she saw.

Turning, Rian frowned at Alexandrine, waiting patiently by the room's door. "It occurs to me that it's always worth asking whether your clever gambit was someone else's move all along."

Alexandrine didn't respond. Princess Heloise said: "Now you're being mysterious."

"I am being annoyed with myself. A short while ago someone very grand called me 'a power in the process of becoming', and I was pleased, and complimented, and did something he wanted. I liked the idea of being the one making the decisions, instead of a tool dragged this way and that by larger forces. But here I am, with a small decision to make, putting off making it because I don't know what will happen next, or how much of this situation has been created. I feel out of my depth, and I've never liked that."

Heloise-D'Argent propped her chin on one hand in a show of boredom. "You make yourself sound most intriguing," she said, in a tone to suggest the opposite.

Rian gazed back at France's Princess Royal, and found herself setting aside calculation in favour of simple fellow feeling.

"Your brother is a chrysalide."

A bald statement that left Princess Heloise utterly still, with not even a flicker of an eyelid to betray her reaction. Rian wondered if it was possible that the princess had already known – but, no, chrysalides were indistinguishable from humans until their wings began to develop.

While she watched, the ribbons and threads around the princess changed – some shrinking away, while others grew longer – and Rian's extra sense brought her a shaft of piercing hurt. Whatever else she felt about the news, the revelation had wounded the Princess Royal. For the silence of her mother, or the loss of her brother?

Rian wondered whether any of it mattered. Was this even the small decision that would have large consequences for the women of France? And, even though she was the daughter of a Frenchman, did Rian truly have any business trying to change a whole country to better suit her own sensibilities?

To better suit Martine and Milo, on the other hand...

"I would like to see your face."

Rian glanced from the princess to Alexandrine, only to find the member of the Tower of Balance had turned her back. Her business was to arbitrate forfeits, not small-large choices.

With a faint shrug, Rian lifted off the white and gold snake mask, and then untied her veil. Princess Heloise tugged free her own, and they looked at each other.

"I do not thank you for this," the princess said. "Or ask how you know it. But I am...but I have heard it." She stood, replacing her veil, and crossed to Alexandrine. "Return me to the assembly hall, if you may." She looked back at Rian. "I will know you again, if I meet you."

And then she was gone. Rian looked at her hands, then carefully replaced veil and mask before finally returning her attention to the mask of a silver lion, almost forgotten on the table.

She picked it up, and lifted it briefly so she could look through its eyes. Martine's future, clear of another threat. Until the next time Henri wanted something from her.

"Is there somewhere I can put this?" she asked, when Alexandrine returned. "I might have forfeits to pay, and I would hate to have come so far only to lose it again."

Alexandrine touched the mask, and it vanished. "Say my name within the Towers and it will return to you."

"Thank you." Rian stood. She thought of asking Alexandrine how much she had known about the Dauphin's two children, and what choice the Court member would have made, if she had been allowed to interfere. Probably Alexandrine had seen it all before, and from the perspective of a century or so it seemed a minor dilemma.

Rian scooped up the remainder of Heloise-D'Argent's Tears, and attached them to her veil.

"Perhaps I will see you again, if I return next century," she said, and was vaguely cheered by the reflection that she would not necessarily outlive everyone she had ever met.

(xii)

If the current fashions lasted into winter, there would be considerable profit to be made in renting coats to the visitors to the Towers. Rian had recovered the rest of her dress, but tissue did little against a chill wind, and she shivered and winced as soon as she stepped from beneath the canopy of the Hall of Balance.

Holding the Mask of Léon firmly, she began to bounce-skip toward the station. It was a tired time of night, an hour or more before dawn, and the island far less crowded than it had been during her arrival mid-evening. A few drifts of weary revellers stumbled toward the entrance to the train station. Others would wait in sheltered seating areas for the return of normal gravity, which would be swiftly followed by the arrival of autocarriages.

Rian was being followed. She knew it even before her perception of the Great Forest strengthened, and she clicked her tongue in exasperation. Probably they hoped for exactly what she carried curled in her right hand: shell-like silvery disks that had been given to her when she left the Towers in exchange for her remaining Tears. She was not overly concerned about defending herself, but a snatch-and-grab might leave the Mask of Léon damaged.

Warmth dropped over her shoulders. Startled, Rian turned to find a black cat mask atop familiar brown curls.

"There was no need to wait out here in the chill, Étienne."

"You know Tante Sabet as well as I, and yet you say that," he said, fussing briefly with the set of his coat around her. "And they wouldn't let me wait *inside* the train station. You have it, then."

Rian glanced down at the Mask of Léon, then said: "Let's get out of the wind."

"I do not ask. Remark on that, for it is a feat of restraint."

Étienne swayed, reoriented himself, and managed a slow wallow toward the train station. The true feat was that he'd managed to stay upright with that much brandy in him.

Even so, Rian no longer felt she was being pursued, and reflected on the value of a visible escort as she steered him down the station ramp and watched him doze during the journey southwest. He roused a little to transfer to an autocarriage, and then slept on her shoulder until they arrived back at the Hotel Lourien.

The front door flew open as they pulled up, and Martine, two porters, and a highly unimpressed Tante Sabet – who was not technically supposed to even know about this expedition, but of course had found out – swarmed over them.

Tante Sabet took one look at the little collection of masks resting on Rian's lap, sniffed, and then told the porters: "Put him in fifteen."

"Good morning, Tante Sabet," Rian said, demurely, but although she earned a second sniff, there was no sharp-tongued lecture. Rian, after all, was a paying guest.

No, this time Tante Sabet would reserve her lectures for Martine, and Martine would accept that as just, and not mind very much. Perhaps she would not even notice.

"You look worn to the bone," Rian said, accepting Martine's hand out of the autocarriage. "A night of worry costs more than a thousand dances."

"I should never have let you go," Martine said, looking Rian up and down as if expecting to discover some great wound from an evening of veiled revelry.

"You know I quite like dancing," Rian reminded her.

Tante Sabet had taken care of paying the driver, and Rian smiled her thanks, since Tante Sabet's disapproval of the Gilded Court was genuine and deeply ingrained. The cost would appear on Rian's bill later, of course, but it was still a large concession.

"We might, I think, need to postpone the review of the twins' birthday arrangements," she said. "Perhaps this evening?"

"Bah. You think I need your advice? Even Prytennian chits are no great mystery."

"You were a girl once, after all," Étienne put in brightly, then lapsed wisely back into unconsciousness as the porters carried him away.

Rian followed their lead, and let Martine help her up the stairs, although she was feeling well enough. Even her feet had stopped hurting.

"You had best get this back where it belongs," she said, pressing the Mask of Léon into Martine's hands as soon as they were in the privacy of her room.

"When you have told me everything," Martine said, firmly, following Rian to her bathroom.

"Everything would take a long time," Rian said, "and you were worried about your supervisor's early arrival at the museum. Besides, all I am going to do is sleep – after I wake whoever is in the pipes room." Ruthlessly she twisted taps and heard, distantly, the banging that had been the bane of many of her nights.

"Did he return it willingly?"

Rian wished she could ignore the small, unhappy question, but she had learned long ago that lying about Henri did not help Martine in the least.

"He had lost it in a game, but I won it back," she said. "Perhaps he would have simply given it up, if he'd still had it. But knowing Henri, I doubt it."

She stripped off her four layers of expensive tissue and draped them over a rail, knowing she couldn't hold back another important detail.

"I extracted a promise from him, under the rules of Forfeit," she said at last, as she stepped into steaming water. "To stay out of Milo's career."

"What?" Martine's face became blank with astonishment. "But...he could do so much for Milo."

"And has made clear, over and again, that he won't help him," Rian said briskly. "If nothing else, this way Milo can stand proudly on his own accomplishments."

One thing Martine had never been was stupid. Nor was she truly blind where Henri was concerned, no matter how many chances she gave him to stand apart from his own history. The bones of her face stood briefly stark, then she bowed her head, and a wing of black hair hid her expression.

"Go put the mask back," Rian said softly.

Martine leaned forward and hugged Rian, tight and fierce, before leaving without another word.

Sighing, Rian slid down in the bath. It always ended with Martine hurt. Nothing Rian had ever done could prevent a devoted heart from eating itself away. And Martine was not even the first person to walk away from Rian that night, concealing wounds with a straight back and set face.

Through rising steam, Rian contemplated her increasing capacity for causing people damage while trying to help them. 'A power in the process of becoming'. Was that even a thing she wanted, when she stepped back from her pride and looked with clear eyes?

She had gained so much in such a short time: godly allegiance, money, position, youth. Great good fortune, or cruel snare? She was undoubtedly being used.

But that did not make her a puppet. Whatever decisions she faced as a result of her new 'advantages', it was still Rian who would make them. Her choices, made wisely or clumsily, guided by her own heart. If there were strings, she would cut them, or grasp them, or simply find her way through them, just as she had the whole of her life.

Rian had always been in the process of becoming. She would grow into power.

Death and the Moon

Eluned Tenning had not expected the trip to France to cure her sister of heart-sickness, but she'd hoped it would buoy her spirits. And that first night in Lutèce – when they had revelled in the wonders of the Towers, and then had a dawn adventure – Eleri had sparked up as any person would.

But it never lasted. Even though they had gone to a dozen museums and galleries full of things that Eleri usually found fascinating, Eluned's sister had barely seemed to be attending. She had dealt with their mass of cousins with distracted politeness, and had not cared about the sudden rearrangement of their plans so their Aunt could visit the Gilded Court. Not even the news of the disappearance of the Princess Royal had caught her interest.

Eluned had tried not to be impatient. It wasn't Eleri's fault she had fallen in love, or that her heart had decided on someone they'd be lucky to meet again, even at the same school. But it was hard not to wish that her sister would just get over it.

On the evening before they were due to return to Prytennia, Eleri settled down after dinner to stare out their hotel room window, and rather than show her frustration, Eluned escaped downstairs to look for a more interesting way to spend the last little bit of the visit to France. In the family-run Hotel Lourien, she almost inevitably would encounter a cousin, and she rather hoped it would be cousin Lotti, who was the most bouncing, cheerful girl Eluned had ever met.

If she had not been so determined to hide her impatience, Eluned would probably not have gone downstairs alone. She had met more than one cousin who was not so enjoyable to talk to as Lotti, and if she happened across cousin Emile, she could not be certain cousin Antoine would arrive a second time to rescue her from that too-friendly arm around her waist.

Thankfully, in the storeroom staff used to take breaks she found one of the younger cousins, Milo, memorising lines for an Aquitanian play, and happily agreed to help him rehearse for the Latin performances.

Eluned had only known Milo a few days, and thought him obliging, hard-working and kind, but he had not stolen all her thoughts, and did not make her want to blush whenever he was around, let alone spend all her time morosely staring at nothing. Even so, she did not move away when Milo's demonstration of how actors faked kisses on stage somehow turned into a not at all pretend kiss.

It tingled to touch someone's tongue with your own. No-one had ever mentioned that. Surprise made Eluned go still.

Milo immediately lifted his head, gave her a concerned look, and said: "Too far?"

"It's all right." Eluned's voice was satisfactorily calm. "It was just different to what I expected."

"You didn't expect me to be so rude as to not ask properly first," Milo said, but then offered her a smile that lit up his odd, angular face. "But me, I am not sorry I was rude, if you are not."

"I'm not," Eluned said, which was true, then added daringly: "At my last school it was such a big thing, to know what kissing was like. I always felt stupid."

"And so you plan to enact a transformation sequence? You shall return to your Prytennia a sophisticate."

Eluned doubted that very much, but she thought that she would be glad, at her new school, to be a person who had at least glimpsed the answer to certain mysteries, even if she still did not properly understand them. All of the descriptions of kissing she had ever read had talked in grand phrases: of being swept away, transported, transfigured. But she was still just Eluned, in a storeroom, with a cousin she had only started to get to know.

"Do you think Tesaire really loves this woman he calls 'the Queen'?" she asked, reaching for the reason they had been talking about kissing in the first place.

Milo's play, *Death and the Moon*, was all about a French conscript in the old Roman Empire's armies. It was full of harsh army discipline, battles with Hellenic rebels, and a mysterious woman whom Milo's character, Tesaire, meets at night.

"There's nothing in the script to suggest his love isn't true," Milo said. "Why do you think it?"

"He's only spoken to her a couple of times. He doesn't know anything about her other than she spends a lot of time staring up at the moon."

"He knows she is beautiful," Milo said. "For some, that is enough."

"But she could be horrid! She won't even tell him her name! And when he warns her his commander is planning to attack the whole district where the rebels are based, all she does is lecture him."

"Because he says he wants to act, to help the Hellenes, for her," Milo said, and then stepped back and spoke in a voice both compassionate and disapproving:

"*My poor boy. Do you think to barter for my affection? Wherever the Fates take you, what point in arriving as anything but your truest self?*"

Eluned blinked, because even though the words were the same she had read to him a short while ago, Milo had somehow made the Queen a much better person. Eluned had read her as ungrateful, but Milo had made her wise.

"That's a little like magic," she said. "I couldn't begin to sound so grand."

"It is not so mysterious," Milo said, laughing. "Here." He pulled a low crate out from beneath one of the shelves.

"Climb up on this. Yes, and now stand very straight – no, put your shoulders back and try and make your neck long."

Eluned obeyed, feeling silly, but he smiled at her encouragingly.

"Now. You are a woman of power, of consequence, and this boy – this puppy – has come to you and asked you to give him a reason. To be his justification. You do not dislike the boy, but you will not be his excuse. So you say..."

"*My...my poor boy...*" Eluned faltered, and felt stupid.

"Deep breath," Milo said. "Keep your neck long, even as you look down at me."

"*My poor boy,*" Eluned said again, and was surprised at the way the words rang out. "*Do you think to barter for my affection? Wherever the Fates take you, what point in arriving as anything but your truest self?*"

"There." Milo beamed up at her. "That is acting. More than words. Being."

"I think I see," Eluned said.

"The Queen – ah, I am so lucky that Sophia Nokoto is to play her. Because, more than beauty, the Queen must have gravitas. It is entirely understandable that Tesaire has fallen in love with her, for she is a being of such power, such aura, that it is impossible to see her and do anything else."

Eluned, who had once met a god with plenty of power and 'aura', did not really agree. Of course, that god had been a deer, most of the time, and quite scary.

"This is important to you somehow, I think," Milo said, unexpectedly. "Why Tesaire loves the Queen."

"I...not really. Not Tesaire." Eluned hesitated, but forged on, because Milo was only a little older, and kind. "My sister, Eleri, she met someone recently. Only once, and they didn't even talk directly, but Eleri hasn't thought of anyone else since. It's like she's been enchanted."

"Le élixir d'amour," Milo said, and Eluned more or less understood what that meant, and nodded.

"I have never experienced that," Milo said, "although I have known people who have. One look, and they are pierced to the core. Of course, for some it is a regular event, and comes and goes like the seasons. Others..." He lifted his hands. "For others, one look is a lifetime, a devotion that nothing will shift. Although...perhaps it is possible that eventually all passions wear thin?" He looked pensive. "You disapprove of your sister's choice, then?"

Eluned shrugged uncomfortably. "It isn't making her very happy. Have you ever been in love, Milo?"

"Oh, yes. Twice. Both times I have been a Tesaire, a puppy, tolerated by a Queen. Not someone to take seriously. And at times I was angry with myself, because it is not enjoyable to be made a puppy, even by your own heart. But..." He took Eluned's hands and traced a few steps of a dance around her. "It thrilled even as it hurt, and though it left the shape of itself behind long after it faded, I do not think myself the worse for it."

"Unlike Tesaire," Eluned pointed out. "If he'd never met this Queen, he wouldn't have ended up dead. Worse, dead as a traitor in Roman territory, so his soul will go to the worst part of the Roman afterlife. All to try to prove himself to someone who doesn't love him back."

"No, no, I don't agree with that interpretation at all. The Queen's words drive Tesaire to prove himself, yes, but only that he is a Frenchman, not a Roman soldier. That he is not someone who will participate in a massacre in the name of the Empire."

"It's really an awful play," Eluned said, wishing he'd been rehearsing something more cheerful. "Tesaire goes through so much after being conscripted, and tries to do the right thing by sending a warning to the rebels – for whatever reason – but ends up walking into an ambush with the rest of the soldiers. Is the audience supposed to be happy that his 'Queen' shows up and kisses him before he dies?"

"Ah, but we haven't finished the final scene." Milo collected his script and handed it back to her, then arranged himself into artful collapse at her feet.

"*My Queen,*" he said, gazing up at her with a mix of defiance and pride. "*This is the last I look upon you. But I look upon you as Tesaire, a free man of France. Remember me well.*"

"*You will not be forgotten,*" Eluned promised, remembering to hold herself as he'd taught her. She stepped down from her crate, but was a little flummoxed as to how to kneel beside him in a grand way. Nor was she entirely sure how a Queen would kiss a dying man, but decided that lightly on the lips would do.

Then she had to stop and look at the script, for this was where they'd paused before for lessons on kissing.

"'*Tesaire rises*'?" she said, reading the pencilled stage directions. "Don't tell me she's god-touched with some sort of healing powers?"

"No, no. It is his spirit we see rising," Milo assured her, lifting himself up as he spoke, as if he was being hauled by ropes. "There is to be a mannequin for his body, hastily inserted from under a nearby bit of scenery. The Queen stands as he rises, and perhaps allows him to touch her arm."

He then dropped back into character, and cried out: "*Grant me the gift of your name, before I am taken!*"

"*I have many names,*" Eluned read. "*I am Sister of the Grain. I am the Moon of the Depths. I am Kore of the Shades. I am She Who Destroys Light.*" Eluned paused, frowning, then read on: "*Come, my Tesaire. I have a place for a true and valiant man of France.*" She lowered the script. "I don't understand. Is she supposed to be a French god?"

Milo laughed. "No. You might recognise her best-known name. All this time, Tesaire has been talking to Persephone."

"Proserpina?"

"That is beauty of it. *Not* Proserpina, no matter what the Romans say. Persephone, Queen of the Dead in her own right. A Hellenic god. To say that the gods of the Hellenes are not gods of Rome using different names, that is one thing that annoys Rome more than anything else. That is why the *Moon* always has at least one performance in Latin. It is a defiance of Rome."

"So he ends up in a Hellenic Otherworld?"

"Yes. And, while being in love is not the reason he chooses to stay true to himself, it does add to his strength, his determination." Milo suddenly covered his face, and then swept his hands back over his hair. "This is such a *large* role. I was so nervous I was ill outside the theatre when they called me back for a second audition. Thank you for reading with me, Eluned."

They read through the final act again, without interruptions. And then Milo asked her, very politely, if she would like to practice kissing a little more, and Eluned decided that she did. No lightning bolts struck, but it was pleasant enough in its way. She would rather see Milo perform, and was sorry she was not staying in France long enough to watch his debut as Tesaire.

Pondering the mystery of why people found kissing so interesting, Eluned went upstairs to find Eleri still sitting at the window of their room, staring out.

Most of the time, Eluned had to admit, Eleri didn't visibly mope. She tended to stay more in the background than Eluned was used to, but there was no visible cloud of gloom. Eluned was just aware of her sister's unhappiness, and hated that she could find no way to make the problem go away.

"We should have a plan," she announced.

Eleri, mind obviously far across the Channel, looked at her slowly.

"For what? Going home tomorrow?"

"For Tangleways. For how we get to meet the Gwyn Lynns again."

Eluned hated herself, then, for the faint shift in Eleri's expression. For the knowledge that she had been too obviously dismissive of what had happened to her sister when she had seen Celestine Gwyn Lynn.

Even if Eluned didn't understand how anyone could love someone they had met once, she knew Eleri. Eleri didn't say things she didn't mean, and Eluned should have given her sister her trust and support, no matter what. Love might bring Eleri strength, or make her a puppy, or just leave her hurt. Eluned couldn't change any of that.

But she could be a true sister, and help her find out.

www.ingramcontent.com/pod-product-compliance
Lightning Source LLC
Chambersburg PA
CBHW060943120626

46557CB00003B/1116